Storie:

MW01705715

DISSIPATION

This book is edited and designed by the Editorial Committee of *Cultural China* series

Managing Directors: Wang Youbu, Xu Naiqing
Editorial Director: Wu Ying
Series Editor: Wang Jiren
Editor: Daniel Clutton
Editorial Assistant: He Siyuan

Text by Tang Ying
Translation by Qiu Maoru

Interior and Cover Design: Wang Wei
Cover Image: Getty Images

ISBN: 978-1-60220-213-9

Address any comments about *Dissipation* to:

Better Link Press
99 Park Ave
New York, NY 10016
USA
or
Shanghai Press and Publishing Development Company
F 7 Donghu Road, Shanghai, China (200031)
Email: comments_betterlinkpress@hotmail.com

Printed in China by Shanghai Donnelley Printing Co. Ltd.

1 2 3 4 5 6 7 8 9 10

DISSIPATION

By Tang Ying

Better Link Press

Preface

English readers will be presented with a set of 12 pocket books. These books contain outstanding novellas written by 12 writers from Shanghai over the past 30 years. Most of the writers were born in Shanghai from the late 1940's to the late 1950's. They started their literary careers during or after the 1980's. For various reasons, most of them lived and worked in the lowest social strata in other cities or in rural areas for much of their adult lives. As a result they saw much of the world and learned lessons from real life before finally returning to Shanghai. They embarked on their literary careers for various reasons, but most of them were simply passionate about writing. The writers are involved in a variety of occupations, including university professors, literary editors, leaders of literary institutions and professional writers. The diversity of topics covered in these novellas will lead readers to discover the different experiences and motivations of the authors. Readers will encounter a fascinating range of esthetic convictions as they analyze the authors' distinctive artistic skills and writing styles. Generally speaking, a realistic writing style dominates most of their literary works. The literary works they have elaborately created are a true reflection of drastic social changes, as well as differing perspectives towards urban life in Shanghai. Some works created by avant-garde writers have been selected in order to present a variety of styles. No matter what writing styles they adopt though, these writers have enjoyed a definite place, and exerted a positive influence, in Chinese literary circles over the past three decades.

Known as the "Paris of the Orient" around the world, Shanghai was already an international metropolis in the 1920's and 1930's. During that period, Shanghai was China's economic, cultural and literary center. A high number of famous Chinese writers lived, created and published their literary works in Shanghai, including, Lu Xun, Guo Moruo, Mao Dun and Ba Jin. Today, Shanghai has become a globalized metropolis. Writers who have pursued a literary career in the past 30 years are now faced with new challenges and opportunities. I am confident that some of them will produce other fine and influential literary works in the future. I want to make it clear that this set of pocket books does not include all representative Shanghai writers. When the time is ripe, we will introduce more representative writers to readers in the English-speaking world.

Wang Jiren

Series Editor

Chapter 1

Nobody came to meet her at the airport.

Su Xiaohui was pushed here and there by the crowds of people coming to meet their relatives or friends. She could see the "blind" people, overwhelmed by the coming reunion. Their eyes were raw with tears of joy or sadness. Such a dramatic scene could only be found here.

Xiaohui seemed to be lost. She tended to avoid any dramatic scenes. Deserted by the crowds, she was standing alone in the center of the lounge, surrounded only by her luggage.

Her parents didn't come to meet her because her mother was hospitalised and her father was looking after her in the hospital. Even when she left Shanghai, she didn't let them see her off at the airport. Her father was 60 at the time, while her mother was 55. She waved to them at the entrance of the alley and jumped on the bus as if it was only a short separation. She was relieved when it started to move.

She looked out of the window and saw a lock of curly hair over her mother's forehead. Her mother looked almost ten years younger than her father. She thought that she would not be coming back in three or four years. Her mother would be about 60 then. A 60-year-old woman would look old and her father, of course, even older. At the thought of this she felt dejected. However, the mixture of laughter and chatting on the bus cleared up her depression.

Ever since she got the entry visa for Malaysia, her 13-square-meter room was transformed into something like a bustling railway carriage. All her relatives and friends came to congratulate her and they seemed more excited than she was. However, she was not so happy about going to Malaysia, for to her it was only a small tropical country covered with forests ... But her relatives and friends seemed more optimistic. They told her that Malaysia was not the final destination, and it only served as a springboard to somewhere else ... anywhere else.

Anywhere else? She had a traveler's visa good for only three months. She shuddered to think what the future would have in store for her. As so many people volunteered to see her off, she had drawn up a list with her mother. To keep the departure a cheerful one she crossed off all the senior relatives from the list. She didn't let her parents go to the airport either and just said good-bye to them in the lane.

Xiaohui had never expected a ten-year separation. She made her decision to go back after seeing the picture of her mother. She was sitting on a bed in a hospital ward, her hair short and completely white. That night Xiaohui drove at 120 kph down an expressway wearing her pyjamas. She burst into tears in the car. She stopped at the roadside and called her father, telling him her plan to return home. She also wrote to tell Qinghua and Zhang Lin about her planned date of return. She was so irritated that she lost her composure. She wanted to tell them that she had been looking forward to the day for ten years. Before she could write anything, her eyes had welled up with tears. She had not written such a candid letter for years. She felt that these few simple words would be a catalyst, unleashing all her pent up emotions.

Many people would come to meet her, more than when she left Shanghai ten years ago. Why not? She had waited for this day the whole ten years. During lonely nights in Kuala Lumpur, alone in the luxury villa, music was her only company. However, music couldn't fill the void in her heart. Her sole solace on those sleepless nights was the coming reunion—after she walked out of the plane and passed through customs she would see familiar faces waiting beyond, waving and holding flowers. A celebration would be held in the airport lounge to welcome her, befitting her long absence from home.

Instead, here she was, standing alone in the center of the airport lounge like an actress abandoned by her audience. The disappointment left her at a loss.

The porter put her luggage in the taxi. Seeing the hesitant expression on her face, the driver asked Xiaohui, "Where to?"

"Take me home!" she said without thinking. Then she mumbled, "I don't even know the way."

The driver stared at her in the mirror. After he started the car he asked, "Do you know which road? Which crossroad?" He looked at her again.

"Do you know Gaolan Road? There's an Eastern Orthodox Church there. Near

Huihai Road and Ruijin Er Road." As she described the location, she came back to reality and regained her mental composure.

"Ok, with those directions I can probably find the place. Don't worry. Even if I can't, I can ask our dispatcher." He switched on the intercom, and then switched it off again immediately. He turned around and cast a smile at her. As his face was obscured by the safety shield, she could only see a blurry face smiling through the dark organic glass. On the airport expressway he spoke, "You've just come back from abroad. I guess it's been years since you left because you're nervous. Why didn't you ask your relatives or friends to meet you?"

"I only have my parents at home," she said, switching into the Shanghai dialect. "Mom is in hospital and Dad keeps her company there. I wrote to my old friends and my relatives, but I'm not sure whether they've received my letters. We lost contact with each other for several years ..." She was unsure why she had given so much away to a stranger. She couldn't help feeling hollow inside. She looked through the window and found the familiar city had become strange to her.

"... Maybe they've moved somewhere else. Many families in Shanghai have been resettled to make way for urban renewal projects. You'll lose contact if you don't keep writing to each other."

She was so worried that she sat straight up. She saw through the safety shield that the driver had a patch of white hair at the back of his head.

The day after her arrival she went to Qinghua's parents' home. The apartment facing Huaihai Road where they once lived was reduced to ruins. Their three big rooms, occupying more than 60 square meters, together with the pharmacy, fruit store and grocery store on the ground floor, had become a big pile of debris on the corner of the street. The sidewalk was covered by dust blown up from the debris, forcing pedestrians to cross the street. It was a scene of complete desolation.

She remembered the summer nights she had spent here. She and Zhang Lin walked around after a thunder shower, the sidewalk covered with wet plane tree leaves. They avoided the crowded Huaihai Road, walking another route along the backstreets until they came to Qinghua's house at the corner of Huaihai Road. The streets they passed were lined up by plane trees. The treetops stood out against a screen of dark blue sky. The blanket of rainwater left the blocks of buildings as lifelike as a forest. Aided by thunder and lightning, the rain purified the air and washed away the worst odours of the city. The smell of cleansed earth emanated from the leaves and soil like flowing streams. The continual flow of ripples left them sensing the existence of shimmering waves even in the middle of the city.

She and Zhang Lin stopped talking and breathed in greedily. Their hearts became as cool and smooth as their clean skin. Being 17, they wore Dacron pants like everyone else. Only the checked short-sleeve blouses drew attention to their youth. They shouted Qinghua's name under her room. Qinghua's parents were senior doctors in the hospital. Her parents turned the corridor into their study and did their reading there every evening. They were so afraid to walk through the closely-guarded passage that they seldom went upstairs. When Qinghua came down, they moved to the entrance of the alley to talk.

During those days when material things were in short supply, they were living a spiritually abundant life. They shouted in unison "Qinghua" and their melodious *putonghua* lingered in the air. Qinghua was their classmate in high school. Probably inheriting the ways of her parents, Qinghua was fond of reading and liked to lecture other people. Qinghua was a voracious novel reader and talented story-teller. They listened to her vivid descriptions of taboo love affairs with mixed feelings of joy and concern. Standing in the bustling street, they found themselves inexplicably agitated for no reason at all.

Her father once told her that it was impossible to rebuild old houses like this. There were not many handsome houses left in Shanghai ... It was easy to demolish an old house no matter how strong its structure was. They adopted the technique of directional blasting. Before you heard the sound the house would cave in like a sandcastle on the beach.

A gust of wind kicked up a cloud of dust from the remains of the building. It was a typical spring wind in Shanghai. The sound of blaring horns from endless lines of traffic grew steadily more annoying. She had to close her eyes.

She sank into a chair holding the phone. She had planned to stay in Shanghai for five days and two had already passed.

The only lead she had was the address of Qinghua's parents. Qinghua had married five years ago and wrote her at the time that she and her husband had no house of their own. Later she revealed that her marriage might not last and her parents' home would be her permanent address ... Xiaohui regretted not answering her letter; at the time she was wearing a bullet-proof jacket every day for fear that her husband's ex-girlfriend would shoot her. She had not received any letters from Qinghua ever since. At the beginning, she and Qinghua sent a greeting card to each other at the end of the year. Later, only she alone sent a greeting card to Qinghua.

Having lost contact with Qinghua, she knew nothing about Zhang Lin. Xiaohui had always been close to her. They lived in the same alley in the childhood and went through school together. They had no secrets. When she was preparing to go abroad, Zhang Lin's family was busy exchanging their antiquated one-room house for a two-room apartment in a faraway district. Zhang Lin promised to write to her after they moved. However, Zhang Lin was hopelessly lazy about writing letters. During her second year in Malaysia, she learned from Qinghua that Zhang Lin was getting married. Xiaohui was leading a desperate life by then—she played mah-jong with rich ladies in a villa at Kuala Lumpur, but she had no money of her own. Fighting back tears, she wrote to her parents, begging them to give two hundred yuan to Zhang Lin on her behalf.

Several weeks later, while at her aunt's house, she received a call from Zhang Lin. In the excitement, and worried about the terrifying phone charges, there was no way they could have a calm conversation. She complained that Zhang Lin didn't write to her and Zhang Lin accused her of bothering her parents with her friend's marriage. Before long the phone line went dead. She was anxious the whole day. That night her aunt told her uncle that she lacked breeding in prattling on the phone in Shanghai dialect. She regretted that she had not asked Zhang Lin enough questions, about her new life. What was her new address? What kind of spouse had this tiny girl with a high IQ picked up?

Afterwards, Zhang Lin called her twice, but it was never at the right time. One call came when she was ready to go out with some of her aunt's friends. The ladies were in the habit of going out together for social activities and bringing their bodyguards with them. While she was talking in the corridor, she worried that the other ladies were getting impatient. Again, she did not find out what she wanted to know. The phone line was cut off as before. She knew that Zhang Lin used a phone card to call her. The next call came when she was not at home. The English-speaking Philippine maid answered the call and must have wasted a lot of Zhang Lin's money. Long-distance calls were charged at 45 yuan a minute. It was once her monthly income. She was so distressed that she wrote to Zhang Lin that night blaming her for being lavish with money ... Absurdly, she sent the letter to Qinghua because she didn't have Zhang Lin's new address.

In her reply, Qinghua passed on Zhang Lin's response: "I spend your two hundred yuan making long-distance calls. You are to blame for sending me the money." Qinghua told her that Zhang Lin's brother quarrelled with his parents over the wedding house. He refused to go to the apartment in the border district. Later they reached a compromise and moved to the ground floor of a *shikumen* style house near their old residence. They got an extra ten square meters by sacrificing the floor with cook appliances and a restroom. Such an exchange was made possible with the help of Zhang Lin's husband, who worked for the housing office. Also with his help, a bathroom was built in the courtyard. Qinghua suspected Zhang Lin of marrying him for the sole purpose of getting a wedding house for her brother. Her husband was only five foot three and balding. Why else would Zhang Lin marry such a man?

Why? That was a reasonable question. Xiaohui was taking an English class at night school. She leant two elbows on the table and held her head in her hands, feeling something stuffed uncomfortably in her stomach. She had a lot on her mind. Oh, housing, housing and housing again. Housing became a terrible frustration to girls like herself and Zhang Lin. When they parted, she told Zhang Lin not to get married until the last moment. What was considered the last moment? They had no answer to this question. She was well aware though that if it was possible she would help Zhang Lin first. She would do her utmost to drag her out of that small factory in Nanshi District. The most important thing was to bid farewell to the life of a philistine who fretted about trifles. Only after she came to Malaysia did she realize that her dream would not come true in the foreseeable future.

She didn't answer Qinghua's letter for a long time. From then on she seemed to become less enthusiastic about writing letters. Zhang Lin never called again, nor did she write. Qinghua never mentioned Zhang Lin's new address in her letters. She never asked for it anymore as if she was avoiding Zhang Lin; or, more exactly, avoiding Zhang Lin's unfortunate and hopeless life. She chose to leave China for the sole reason of avoiding this kind of fate, didn't she?

"You will lose contact if you don't keep writing to each other." Xiaohui couldn't accept his absurd logic. She had been certain that she would find them when she came back. She could only pour out her true feelings about the past ten years to Zhang Lin and Qinghua, her two closest friends. Otherwise, why would she bother coming back?

After she married a Chinese Malaysian 20 years elder than her, she realized that she had set out on a long, lonely journey. Her parents didn't write to her for six months. Both of them were decent people who never went beyond what was proper. How could they accept the fact that a widower around the age of the "male menopause" had married their pretty young girl? "You don't live in a feudal society. Nobody has forced you and you should not belittle yourself," her father scolded her. She was so angry that she hung up on him. What an ignorant and stupid man! Her husband was one of the richest men in Kuala Lumpur! She had waited three years for his proposal. In an urgent letter her father told her that happiness couldn't be bought. (Xiaohui laughed quietly to herself at this overblown, empty talk.) He wrote, "What's the use of so much money? We won't spend a penny of yours." (She couldn't help shaking her head. She knew her father would not ask her for money. But she herself needed the money and could her parents support her?) When she read the words "How can we explain your behavior to our relatives," she tore up the letter angrily. All of them can go to hell! Damn it! Do we live just to make them happy?

During the long period of separation, her parents couldn't resist yearning for their daughter. Seven years after she went to Kuala Lumpur, they applied for an entry visa to visit her. After staying with her for less than six months, they were eager to return to Shanghai. They were not used to living a life of luxury on someone else's money. Her parents were working people, supporting themselves their whole life. Whenever they sat in a spacious reception hall, hundreds of square meters large, they would feel ashamed of themselves. Her mother was worried about the recurrence of her heart trouble. The more you were afraid, the stronger the disease took hold. Several visits to the hospital cost them thousands of dollars. They were guilty about spending their son-in-law's money. Her father complained that life abroad was not healthy. Her mother said year round summer would shorten her life. Xiaohui began to realize: "The time wheel cannot reverse, and what's done can't be undone." Her marriage had created an unbridgeable gap between herself and her parents.

During the periods of separation, they were longing to see each other. When she called them, her mother used to ask, "Why can't you come back home? It only takes a few hours to fly back. Why?" Before her marriage everything seemed to be hanging in midair. She still felt like she had not achieved anything meaningful. How could she return home with nothing tangible to show for her long absence?

Dramatic changes took place in her life after marriage. She felt as if she were waking from a dream and found all the closed doors were now open to her. She herself, not her husband, was to blame ... As one of the richest men in Kuala Lumpur, her husband was the prince charming of many distinguished, unmarried women. They admired his gentle and refined manner. However, he fell head over heels in love with Xiaohui. During that period, he devoted all his precious free time to her. They seldom saw each other though. Lying on the bed, they had a heart-to-heart talk over the phone every night. His gentle voice became part of her life, an oasis in a vast expanse of scorching desert.

At the very moment she found herself alone and depressed by her bleak future, a friend, a rich friend, came to her side. She dragged herself out of her self-pity when she learned of his feelings for her.

In retrospect, she didn't expect too much from him at the beginning. If it had not been for a permanent residence card, she would not have married him. They might have a romantic relationship and she might be his appreciative lover. Of course, he would give her money from time to time. There might be a blank space between them. She would be an idiotic woman ... Why not, if stupidity could relieve her sufferings.

Sometimes, life can be like sitting on top of a slide. Before you know it, you slide down into the pool of mud at the end of the slide. She was sitting on the slide of marriage and slid into the pool of truth. Her husband was a renowned entrepreneur. However, the wealthiest and most refined gentleman in Kuala Lumpur could only nominally call her "wife." On their wedding night, he admitted the truth: he could give her everything except sexual love. She was more embarrassed than him. He thought she was prepared to accept a barren marriage. He embraced her in a tender manner and said, "We have to make sacrifices. I sacrificed my health for our family. You will sacrifice some happiness for the sake of your future ... " What a bitter irony! She seemed to have received a beautifully-wrapped big box as a gift. She opened the wrapping paper layer after layer and found nothing inside. She seemed to have entered a big mansion and passed through the hall into the inner chamber, only to find herself locked in an empty house. She asked herself repeatedly: why don't you run away? But how could she return in defeat? Calm and self-possessed, she took up the position of a rich man's wife. People found that her husband brought her to his company. Later they became partners, and she turned out to be his commercial companion in its true sense. The void in her heart at night seemed insignificant and only the company's interests became important.

The tender night time conversations

and romantic feelings between them came to a stop after they got married. Any romance, even an imagined romance (sometimes she thought she must be mad) was nothing compared with the great cause of his distinguished family. As a woman, she had nothing. She enjoyed no sex or the comfort of her own child. She gained a permanent residence card. She became the housewife of the distinguished Ye family. She owned several villas. Gone forever was the girl of *tingzijian* (a kind of small between-floor back rooms in Shanghai)! Her memory became a dark shadow looming now and then on the horizon of her colorful life.

The imprint of her former life was impossible to erase. She had lived through those turbulent years when everything was in short supply. Tormented by desire and frustration, she formed lavish spending habits. What she liked most was housing because it had been the focus of her fears. Reading real estate ads became her hobby. She bought and sold houses frequently as she couldn't own all the beautiful villas. Her hobby turned out to be her talent. Since the Ye family appreciated this talent of hers, she was assigned the job of doing real estate business for the company. She was delighted to have her own career. She now had a convenient excuse for leaving early in the morning in her red sports car and returning late at night.

However, it was not enough to have a career. Like many other rich ladies, she spent a couple of hours every evening in the fitness center and beauty salon. At the age of 35, she was proud of her slim and supple figure as well as her soft and ivory-smooth skin. She examined her naked body in the mirror. Excited by her unrestrained anticipation, she immediately covered herself with a soft bath towel. At 9 o'clock every night she and her husband had dinner at the same restaurant. After dinner her husband would have some entertaining to do, and she would drive herself home. They slept in separate bedrooms. She never stayed up late, so she didn't know when her husband came home. She installed a hi-fi system in her bedroom and music became her nightly companion. While listening to the melodies, she was intoxicated by its poetic beauty. But sometimes she sensed the meaninglessness and cruelty of her life. She felt it all passing her by. Leaving the music playing loudly, she rushed out of her bedroom and drove onto the expressway. She howled like an animal while speeding along. After that she would have a sound sleep. She didn't ponder her inner feelings, unless she had to deal with physiological symptoms, such as her desire to howl.

She asked her husband when they would go back to Shanghai. Her husband said they would go after they had settled the most pressing matters facing them. She waited year after year. She found she was using up tomorrow's pleasure while she waited. Or maybe she was doubtful about whether she would be able to feel any pleasure when she went back home. The serious illness of her mother forced her to come back.

On her way home, in addition to worrying about her mother, she was obsessed by the idea of seeing Qinghua and Zhang Lin. They had lost touch with each other with everything still uncertain. If she didn't see them this time, she would be devastated.

Her father was dozing on the sofa. The sports news was on TV. Xiaohui was anxious and afraid. Time was going by. Three days, three precious days, had passed. She still had no information on Zhang Lin and Qinghua. She was afraid that she might lose them forever.

When she was ready to go back to her hotel at 8 o'clock, the coming of an unexpected visitor changed everything. After she turned off the TV and made the bed for her father, she put on her jacket and picked up her handbag. She was about to leave when she heard someone stop at the door. The door was unlocked and when it opened a woman's face appeared.

"Xiaohui, do you still recognize me?" the woman said, stepping inside.

Of course she recognized her. She was

familiar with Zhen Zhen's plump nose, shrivelled teeth, angular lips and crisp voice. If she had not had a generous figure and a fat chin, had not curled her hair or worn a suit, Zhen Zhen would have been a pretty girl. Xiaohui was doing subtraction in her head for Zhen Zhen. In the past few years she had been doing this to herself. She looked at herself in the mirror: minus freckles on the nose, minus the slight wrinkles round her eyes, minus the intangible tiredness on the surface of her skin ... In order to do subtraction, she went to the beauty salon frequently. However, ageing, just like spring rain, would ravage the earth of youth overnight.

"It's 17 years since we last met! We had just graduated from high school. I went to another province. You haven't changed a bit you know!" Zhen Zhen was as talkative as before, but her facial expression revealed her empty flattery.

She and Zhen Zhen kept up an open or veiled rivalry ever since they entered kindergarten. Zhen Zhen was bright and clever. Xiaohui was pretty and cute. As both of them were the darlings of their teacher, they strove to win more favor. They lived in the same alley and knew each other's background inside out. That's why they avoided meeting each other and never played together. But at that moment, Xiaohui was delighted to see this uninvited guest and said, "I didn't expect you would come. I haven't met many of my old friends since I came back ..."

Her voice sounded very unfamiliar to Zhen Zhen. Her subdued tone, mature and charming, revealed nothing of her true feelings. Sitting steadily in the only mahogany chair with her arms crossed in front of chest, she looked graceful and languid. Zhen Zhen was embarrassed to see such arrogant and unapproachable beauty.

"I was so excited when I learned that you were coming back. It's been such a long time. If my daughter hadn't had a fever, I would have come to the airport to meet you."

Xiaohui felt a lump in her throat at these words. To hide her emotions, she got up and offered Zhen Zhen the chocolate and nuts she had bought in Malaysia. Her father woke up and said, "Nowadays, only Zhen Zhen comes to keep us company. Her daughter is ten years old. She has a great talent for the piano." With a sudden sigh, he added, "What good fortune Zhen Zhen has!"

Xiaohui glimpsed at her father. He

was lighting a cigarette. Hearing his veiled criticism of Xiaohui, Zhen Zhen said with a hearty laugh, "Who has good fortune? Xiaohui is a foreigner now. She owns several villas and she's rich. Compared with her I am nothing." There was no sting in her remark. She seemed to be in high spirits.

Xiaohui felt apprehensive about where the conversation seemed to be going. Zhen Zhen suddenly changed the topic, "Xiaohui, I'm a housewife now. When we were young, we were striving for good marks at school. How has it all turned out? I have to stay at home looking after children." She was still in high spirits and didn't regret losing opportunities. Xiaohui still remembered how the girls at high school ridiculed the work of a housewife.

Without any prompting from Xiaohui,

Zhen Zhen said, "I live a pretty uneventful life, but I'm happy enough because my husband listens to me. We worked together in the mine in Shanxi. He became my boyfriend. I told him to apply for a place in Shanghai when he took the University Entrance Exams. I wouldn't talk to him about marriage until he got a place. As soon as he was admitted, I married him. I asked for sick leave and stayed in his parents' home in Shanghai. They lived in a *shikumen* house, and life without sanitary appliances was sheer suffering. I insisted on enduring life there instead of moving back to my parents' home. I thought I'd put a little pressure on him. As a straight-A student, he was assigned a job in Shanghai after graduation. I got myself officially registered as a Shanghai citizen again. Then I gave birth to a baby and I hated the idea of working even more. I had no professional qualifications, so it was difficult to find a decent job. My husband told me to stay at home and that he would provide for me ..." Without a break, she gave a brief account of her ups and downs. She seemed quite satisfied with the life she was living. Xiaohui was jealous of her just as she had been many years ago when Zhen Zhen always outdid her at school.

"Zhen Zhen's husband is the assistant general manager of a joint venture." Her father added, "He is chauffeured to work by a company car. He goes abroad on business several times a year. They gave him a three-bedroom apartment in Hongqiao Development Zone. Do you know how much it costs? More than 400,000 yuan. What's the good of going abroad for a man like him, who is so successful at home?" He gave Xiaohui a sharp look, seeming to reproach her for something. Zhen Zhen said with a smile, "Come on, Chinese people are no match for foreigners. Xiaohui has seen the world but I'm just an ordinary woman. I stay at home to teach my daughter the piano. Housework is done by a maid." She showed off her hands, saying, "Xiaohui, as you know, I didn't do well in music class. I never dreamt that I would play the piano thirty years later!" Her hands looked plump, even fat. She was certainly not a woman who did household chores. Xiaohui changed the topic of conversation abruptly, "Zhen Zhen, I can't find Zhang Lin or Qinghua."

To her considerable surprise, Zhen Zhen told her that she often met Zhang Lin, who was the owner of a flower shop. "Of course, you'll meet Qinghua there."

Her face darkened. "She is too presumptuous. We don't talk to each other anymore ..."

Xiaohui's joyous exclamation cut her short. She rushed over to hug Zhen Zhen and said, "Zhen Zhen, I thought I wouldn't see them again!"

In a gloomy mood Zhen Zhen struggled out of her embrace. It was the first time tonight that Xiaohui was not her usual self. All of a sudden, Zhen Zhen's delights in getting the upper hand over her melted into thin air.

Chapter 2

In the hotel room that morning Xiaohui tried on everything she had brought with her. Finally she chose jeans and a white cambric blouse. Though expensive, the clothes were simple and restrained. She liked this look. With her elegant short hair, she looked fresh and engaging. Her husband praised her for her taste in clothing—low-key but original. She felt that her shrewd choices were a reflection of her worldly experience. How could her husband understand this?

She took off the diamond earrings and wedding ring. She wanted to remove anything that might alienate her from her old friends. However, once they met each other, she was painfully aware of the time that had passed.

She left the hotel and went back to her parents' home. She deliberately avoided meeting them in the spacious hotel room, because she wanted to create the right atmosphere of familiarity. She was restless the whole morning. Zhen Zhen promised that they would come before noon. To calm herself down, she began watching a film and soon dozed off. She was disturbed by someone calling her name. She had experienced the same feeling at high school. While she was taking a nap at noon, Zhang Lin would come to call her for afternoon classes.

She reluctantly opened her eyes and saw Qinghua taking off her shoes at the door.

"I've waited for you for the whole morning!" she complained, as if this one morning was more important than ten years. She was sometimes clumsy expressing herself.

Qinghua, who was tall and stout during their school days, had become thinner and prettier. Her single-fold eyelids were painted and her red lips were carefully drawn. Her well-preserved face looked soft and radiant. She knew how to choose appropriate clothing for different seasons. Her white cambric short-sleeved jacket was complemented by a close fit T-shirt. In the late spring weather she looked neat and stylish. Qinghua found a seat and sat down. She raised her head and looked at Xiaohui with a slightly sardonic smile.

"You rich ladies don't know the misery of us office workers. We have no time for anything except work. Today is the editorial department weekly meeting. I made an excuse and sneaked off to come and see you."

"I'm sorry. I thought ... I didn't realize you had office hours to keep ..." She was filled with remorse, but what for?

"I don't have fixed hours in my job, but I'm moonlighting, so I'm always busy during the day."

"You're so beautifully dressed that you look like a woman of both money and leisure. How can you take a bus with this attire on?" Xiaohui joked.

Qinghua was pleased by her flattery and said with a smile, "I am not as shabby as you expected. How can my Chinese brands compare with what you wear? Your Armani outfit must cost thousands of dollars. That's beyond my wildest dreams."

With a guilty conscience she forced a thin smile. Was "Armani" a gap between them? But Qinghua was composed and said, "Xiaohui, money can change a woman. It has transformed a pretty girl of humble birth ten years ago into a lady in a rich and powerful family. If I had met you in the street, I would have been ashamed to say hello ..." She looked around and said, "Why haven't you bought a house for your parents? It seems that only this room hasn't changed in the past ten years." Xiaohui found it difficult to adapt herself to this kind of comments. A serene smile was her best defence.

"Qinghua, their ideas are still as dated as they were a decade ago. They feel guilty if they have money. They are ashamed of my marriage, especially my father. He thought I married for money. That's why he was against me buying a house for him ..."

"What's wrong with getting married for money? If nothing else, money can at least give you a decent life. A poor man is not necessarily more virtuous than a rich man."

Xiaohui felt relieved by Qinghua's remarks and couldn't help laughing. It seemed to her that Qinghua's cynicism arose from men. She was listening attentively to her story when Zhen Zhen and her daughter came in shouting and laughing.

Zhen Zhen had booked a table at a restaurant and notified Zhang Lin to go there directly. Qinghua flatly turned down her invitation, saying that she had to attend a working lunch. She left even without saying good-bye to Zhen Zhen and her daughter. Xiaohui followed her downstairs. Upset by their relationship, she blamed Zhen Zhen at heart for trying to meddle. But she said to Qinghua, "I would not have met you without her help, so ..."

Qinghua cut her short, "I'm really busy. I'm teaching a foreigner Chinese on top of my two jobs. Zhang Lin is busy too. She's renovating her flower shop and she's planning to open a fast-food restaurant. Her husband is so stressed out that he's losing his hair. Of course, we'll meet before you leave ..."

They would meet only once more? She thought they should be together every day. She stopped Qinghua at the entrance of the alley, saying, "Yesterday I went to your old house only to find it in ruins. Do you remember how often we used to chat there? I've been looking forward to this moment for the past ten years ..." Tears were streaming down her cheeks.

On the spur of the moment Qinghua took out a business card from her pocket. She didn't provide the card earlier because she knew Zhang Lin was against it and also because of her selfishness. She was moved by Xiaohui's loneliness.

Xiaohui wiped her tears before she looked up at Qinghua and said, "Thank you, Qinghua. I can't thank you enough."

She held Qinghua's hand. Qinghua found her fingers were cold and this coldness would linger in her memory for a long time.

Zhang Lin came in as if she had just been on a long journey. In Xiaohui's mind, Zhang Lin looked like a middle-aged housewife she had seen ten years before. Her dry curly hair looked like a bird's nest. Old fashioned clothing was hanging over her because she was reduced to skin and bones. Her facial skin was so rough that a few pigmented spots appeared. She was just a dust-covered, grey-haired working woman.

Xiaohui, Zhen Zhen and her daughter had waited at the restaurant for Zhang Lin for about an hour. When they saw Zhang Lin in such a state, they were annoyed. "How come you let yourself look like this?" Xiaohui reproached her.

"I was cooking a meal for the workers," she said apologetically. "When the house is renovated and the restaurant is open, it will be much better."

Would it be better? She had known many proprietors of Chinese restaurants. They spent their whole lifetime in the kitchen. They were even worse off than their employees, because they had no days off. It was only natural that they begrudged spending the fruits of their toil.

Zhang Lin said, "I always said to myself that I would write to you when I had time. It was dragging on and on and ten years has passed. I was eager to meet you. There was a traffic jam, so I took a motorcycle taxi. Oh, you are still so pretty!"

"People are living a different life abroad, even in such a small country as Malaysia. I'd never heard of it," Zhen Zhen said rashly. "Zhang Lin is too hard-working. When she took over the flower shop, she had her hands full. She had to take care of everything in the shop. How could she keep herself young?"

It was annoying to listen to Zhen Zhen. Xiaohui looked at Zhang Lin and didn't know what to say. She and the fashionable Qinghua seemed to belong to two different generations. But Qinghua had her own troubles—divorce and an affair with a married man. Zhen Zhen had talked in detail about Qinghua's life while they were waiting for Zhang Lin. Zhen Zhen played the role of a narrator, while Xiaohui's best friends didn't seem to have much time for her.

After the meal, Xiaohui insisted on seeing Zhang Lin home. She thought by getting rid of Zhen Zhen, she and Zhang Lin could speak freely to each other. However, when they got into the taxi, they lapsed into silence. Finally, Xiaohui had to say something.

"Zhang Lin, your husband should not make you slave away like this."

"He's not to blame. He tries his best to let me live a comfortable life, but he isn't capable of it. Unlike you and Qinghua, I'm not seeking any great fortune. I'm satisfied with a loving husband and a promising son. My son is a fourth-grader now. He's a leader of the Young Pioneers. He is a conscientious child. I never need to spend time supervising his studies."

Xiaohui responded with a casual nod. As she herself had no children, she didn't care much for someone else's child. But she was touched by Zhang Lin's sense of pride and sighed softly, "It's true, everyone lives their own life. Other people's perceptions are usually wrong. Sometimes, you may envy someone's lifestyle, but that very person may not like his way of life at all ..."

The taxi was crawling like a tortoise

and finally came to a stop. The driver lowered the window and poked his head out. The sounds of the bustling streets seeped into the car.

Zhang Lin turned her head and stared at her with deep affection, "Xiaohui, does he ... treat you well?"

Her forehead against the window, Xiaohui stared outside and didn't reply.

When the driver closed the window, it was silent in the car. The driver saw in the mirror two women lost in thought.

Zhang Lin's shop was formerly a western-style house, occupying over thirty square meters. The ground floor was piled up with cement, sand and other building materials. The original interior decoration was removed. What remained was an exquisitely carved ceiling, an equally well carved oak door and a wide wooden windowsill. Zhang

Lin told her the wedding room given to her husband was a *tingzijian* not far away from her parents' house. Five years later this room was assigned to them, only two blocks away from her parents' house. Zhang Lin sighed with a smile.

"We endured five years and the days of bitter hardship were gone forever." Xiaohui didn't respond and Zhang Lin added with a smile, "I remember Qinghua said a long time ago that we should find a husband in this neighborhood, between Fuxing Road in the south and Changle Road in the north ..."

"She was too sure of herself," Xiaohui said with a frown, "I heard that she married to a villager from the northeast. She forced him to live in her parents' home. She almost lost a house when she got divorced."

"Zhen Zhen didn't know the truth,"

Zhang Lin calmly explained. "The northeasterner was a doctor who got a teaching job in his own university after graduation. He was a handsome young man and would have been a fine match for Qinghua. But he couldn't bear living with Qinghua's parents. With them it was all rules: 'you're not supposed to make any noise while you eat;' 'you can't eat anything before your parents have had some.' After three months they moved out and rented a farmer's house. Qinghua is not one for housework and their life was miserable. They were so different in their way of living and in their interests ..."

"It seems to me she had a premonition when she made the remarks," Xiaohui cut in. Noticing that Zhang Lin was not pleased by this, Xiaohui added, "At least you've been surrounded by what you're familiar with for the past 30 years."

After a moment of silence, Zhang Lin said, "I didn't marry him for his house. I was grateful to him for giving me help when I needed it. As you know, my brother is a disloyal son. My mother has suffered a lot because of him. My father was no better when he was alive. Instead of earning money to support the family, he only knew how to spend. My family background taught me a lot. It was really great of him to take care of me so well ..."

Their conversation continued over the shrill noise of the workers in the next room.

Then she followed Zhang Lin upstairs.

The attic above the room served as Zhang Lin's bedroom. As it was only about a meter in height, the wooden bed frame was put directly on the ground. A child wearing the insignia of the Young Pioneers lay on the bed reading. In spite of the jarring noise made by the workers downstairs, he was absorbed in his book. Xiaohui remembered that Zhang Lin was also the chief leader of the Young Pioneers in elementary school. She was so fast finishing her homework that even the boys admired her. The Cultural Revolution began that year. She and Zhang Lin studied at the same high school. After graduation she stayed in Shanghai, while Zhang Lin went to a farm.

She gave a red envelope containing a hundred dollars to Zhang Lin's son. The boy had a crimson face that looked like his mother's. He looked up at Zhang Lin. Xiaohui turned expectant eyes on her. "Thank your aunt," she said.

The boy repeated his mother's words

respectfully. Xiaohui was so filled with affection for the boy that she rushed over to embrace him. She mumbled to him, "After you graduate from high school, I will see to it that you are enrolled in an American university."

When they walked downstairs from the attic, Zhang Lin wanted to say good-bye to Xiaohui. She said, "Go back home, I'll come and see you tonight."

Xiaohui seated herself on a low stool near the flower stand outside the shop. As the street crossed Huaihai Road, it was crowded with people. There was a bus stop in front. Xiaohui was dazzled by the hustle and bustle of the streaming traffic and the flow of pedestrians. Zhang Lin joined her, sitting on a low bamboo chair. The two women made quite a contrast, one beautifully attired and the other dishevelled, as they sat and had a heart-to-heart talk. Passers-by looked at them in surprise. They didn't care. Xiaohui took out a business card and showed it to Zhang Lin, "Qinghua gave me Cheng Cong's address. Only Qinghua would act like that."

Zhang Lin stared at her with her big black eyes. A few seconds later she shook her head, saying, "I won't stop you if you make up your mind to see him."

"Even if you wanted to, could you stop me?" Xiaohui said with a sneer. "Even my parents can't stop me. They did their utmost to sabotage my marriage. Were they successful?" She was feeling provocative and couldn't hold her tongue.

"That's why I kept silent. I went to the post office to make long-distance calls. I dialled your number and hung up every time. I knew if I wanted to stop you, I had to go to Kuala Lumpur." The cool tone, which was typical of Zhang Lin, reflected her unusual intelligence, hidden beneath her unkempt appearance. "I was sure I'd be able to stop you if we talked face to face. But I couldn't go to Kuala Lumpur."

"Don't be so sure of yourself, Zhang Lin. My marriage is actually the best thing that's ever happened to me."

She shouted in a fit of pique, "I won't live a miserable life like yours. In the past I had nothing, but now I can get anything I want. Why should you stop me from leading a happy life?"

Zhang Lin nodded her head, saying, "I gradually came round to your idea. That's why I'm against your meeting Cheng Cong again. Since your marriage is a happy one, you ought to show some appreciation for it. After so many years you should've learned to cherish what is valuable!" She became so angry that she snatched the card from Xiaohui's hand and tore it into pieces.

On the contrary, Xiaohui calmed down.

"You're too extreme. Cheng Cong had nothing to do with my marriage. You have more old-fashioned ideas than my parents ..."

Zhang Lin cut her short and said with a sneer, "You're but deceiving yourself, Xiaohui. And Qinghua, too. Since you are a glib talker, you think you're capable of convincing others. But can you change the facts? Everyone has to live her own life. A self-deceiver will get what she deserves."

Xiaohui got worked up and said, "What do I deserve? What do you mean? Whenever we meet problems, you always think you are the only one who knows how to solve them. Where were you when I wanted to talk to you? You didn't write me a word, as if we were strangers ..." Xiaohui suddenly checked herself. How could she quarrel with her old friend as what she used to do after a ten year separation?

"We were thousands of miles apart. How could a letter solve anything? It takes time to argue something out. I was exasperated whenever I thought of writing a letter. So I gave up writing altogether. But whenever I went to the Jade Buddha Temple I always burned incense and made a wish for you ..." Zhang Lin blew her nose with a tissue.

They looked at the street scene silently. After a while Zhang Lin said, "In the third year after you left, Cheng Cong came back and asked me about you. I didn't tell him much. I didn't want to, because you weren't doing so well at the time. I really hoped you could show off to him!"

Xiaohui said with a long sigh, "If I had got in touch with him at the time, things might have been totally different ..." She covered her face with her hand before she finished speaking. Tears were flowing out of the crevices of her fingers.

When a bus finally arrived, people scrambled to get on. They were packed in like sardines and a couple of passengers were hung outside the door. Stunned pedestrians stopped to watch with open mouths.

After she regained her composure and wiped off her tears, Xiaohui fixed her eyes on the stationary bus. After it started to move, Zhang Lin said, "That year Cheng Cong came back to China for medical treatment. He wasn't capable of doing anything. He felt life was boring." Seeing Xiaohui knitting her brows, she continued, "Cheng Cong didn't come back again until the year before last. He'd changed so much for the better. He'd become an investor, doing business mainly in Dalian. He often came back to Shanghai. He asked me twice for your address. I didn't give it to him though. Then he went to see Qinghua. Qinghua ignored him to start with. But she finally gave in because she was so infatuated with him." She glanced at the sky in a dark mood. Then she forced a smile, but it couldn't hide her boundless grief. Her melancholy face made a deep impression on Xiaohui's mind.

"I told her, you can be friendly with

Cheng Cong, but don't give him Xiaohui's address, and don't let him bother Xiaohui."

"What did she say?"

"She said, 'Of course not. If they get in touch with each other, he will certainly brush me aside.'"

"She still gave me his address."

"That's her nature."

Xiaohui was lost in thought. She reminisced about the complicated relationship between them. When she and Cheng Cong fell head over heels in love with each other, Qinghua maintained her dignity in silence. For quite a long period of time she was not aware of Qinghua's feelings. When the three of them were together, she monopolised the conversation and only talked about Cheng Cong. Her immaturity must have bored the others to tears. That's why

Qinghua chided her for "being foolish with an intelligent appearance." But when Cheng Cong dumped her and went abroad, Qinghua was both indignant and sentimental. Her broken heart was soothed by Qinghua's thoughtful behaviors.

She and Cheng Cong spent the whole summer swimming at dusk. Cheng Cong was not good at swimming. He only wanted to be with her during his remaining days in Shanghai. That lasting scorching summer was disagreeable to local people. Xiaohui was covered in sweat the whole day. She often retreated to the pool to keep cool. The people at the shallow end stood thick as a forest. Cheng Cong usually floated along in the deep end. One day, Xiaohui was standing beside the pool in her bathing suit. To Cheng Cong's mind, she was as beautiful as a mermaid. However, he had got his visa from the US consulate and had already booked an air ticket. Helplessly, he saw his mermaid jump into the water and swim away from him.

The first autumn rain drove away the scorching heat as well as the enthusiastic swimmers. Cheng Cong already sat in the lecture hall of an American university. She still went to the deserted pool. She plunged to the bottom of the deep end. All her energy flowed out of her into the light blue water. It was not a sudden blow. Cheng Cong dragged things out before he made his final decision. When she climbed out of the water, she saw Qinghua covered with a bath towel. She was sitting beside the pool crying. She was wiping her tears with her wet hand ...

She insisted upon swimming in autumn and winter. Every weekend Qinghua came back from the university and met her at the swimming pool. Qinghua had no love for sports. She caught a cold while sitting beside the pool. She suffered from chronic rhinitis and looked pale during the cold season.

Zhang Lin's father breathed his last that winter. She looked haggard and emaciated at the funeral. Only Xiaohui herself looked healthy and strong. As a girl suffering from disappointment in love, she ought to be ashamed of her sound health. Her cheeks were glowing and her legs were strong and shapely. This was the payback for all her exercise during the winter. She was very proud of her figure and she knew she was attractive to men. The next spring, she fell in love again. At the same time, Qinghua was engaged in writing sad poems on campus.

The cold season she had spent in the swimming pool remained fresh in her memory. Standing on the high diving platform and enveloped by the slightly biting wind after the autumn rain, she made a graceful twist in the air and dived into the pool. The warm water was as soft as a cotton quilt covering her body and soul. In the piercing winter, the moment she jumped into the warm water, she still shivered with cold. Then she exerted herself to make strokes not only with her arms, but with every part of her body. In this way she put her affection for Cheng Cong behind her. When she put on her clothes and walked out of the swimming pool, she found the yellow leaves of the plane trees withering. People braced themselves against the buffeting wind. She lifted up her head in a light-hearted mood and let the wind blow her hair everywhere.

Advancing against the piercing cold, she sensed her youth and vigour. Twenty-two was a perfect age—a combination of past experience and a bright future. Her disappointment in love became a memory as distant as the scorching summer. As time went by, the feelings she had in each moment led to one love affair after another. Just as Qinghua said, a pretty girl could live a carefree life. The past would start to catch up with her in the lonely days to come though.

Xiaohui was lost in thought. When she woke up, Zhang Lin was busy working in the shop. Dusk was approaching, bringing welcome relief to the extreme heat of the daytime. The setting sun shone its brilliance along half the street. Disturbed by the dazzling light reflected from the shop windows, Xiaohui shaded her eyes with her hand. When she felt the chill in the evening of late spring, she suddenly thought of her mother lying in the ward. She said good-bye to Zhang Lin.

"Anyway, you should make time for us three to have a comfortable chat somewhere quiet. I've been looking forward to this for so long. I have to leave Shanghai in a couple of days ..." she complained in a sentimental tone. When she saw Zhang Lin with disheveled hair wearing a greasy apron, spreading two wet hands and splashing soy accidentally on her nose, she felt bored. She waved good-bye to her.

Zhang Lin called her and said, "If you have time, please go and visit Zhijun's mother. His family are being relocated and his mother came to say good-bye to me the other day. When flowers were cheap in spring, she often came to buy flowers and asked about you."

Was she really that graceful woman with deep set eyes and a high nose? If she had not been Zhijun's mother, they would have been close friends. Ten years had passed and she was over 50. She was still fond of flowers. With the curtains drawn together all the year round, her west side room was furnished with a whole set of mahogany furniture. In such a crowded room, it was difficult to find a suitable place for her lovely china vase.

"How is Zhijun? Is he all right?" she asked with a hint of concern in her voice. She thought that she should have forgotten him long ago, but the mention of his name brought memories rushing back to her, so real that he seemed like part of her family.

Zhang Lin gave her a sly smile. Xiaohui didn't like her smile. It seemed to mock her. She preferred to be ignorant of what was behind it. Xiaohui suddenly felt the distance between them.

Chapter 3

She went to Zhijun's home that night.

The walls of his alley had been demolished and it was shaded by high-rise buildings. She walked through the rubble and found her way to the house. At the entrance, she was confronted by a panel of doorbells. Xiaohui was afraid of pressing the wrong bell. When she was on intimate terms with Zhijun, he gave her the key to his house. Every day when Zhijun's mother went to work, she and Zhijun did whatever they liked and threw all caution to the wind. Those were the most decadent days of her life. She asked for sick leave and spent days fooling around with Zhijun. His mother didn't intervene. She welcomed Xiaohui, or to be more exact, all Zhijun's friends. She enjoyed the liveliness they brought. Her west side room was darkened by drawn curtains, just like the overcast sky. She was afraid of living along in the deserted room. Xiaohui believed it was out of this fear that she went out on dates in her middle age.

Xiaohui walked to and fro downstairs. The back door was tightly shut. Only by shouting Zhijun's name could they hear her from the third floor. Xiaohui was on edge. If Zhijun walked out to meet her, it would make her return worthwhile. There and then, her hidden desire seized her and she wanted to shut the back door and rush up the stairs just as she did ten years ago ... She and Zhijun had spent their days in continuous lust. Her desire never abated until she got the visa.

She was not courageous enough to call his name. Intuition told her Zhijun didn't live here anymore. Would she look for Zhijun as eagerly as Cheng Cong had looked for her? She leant against the door for a moment before she knocked at the door calmly. A woman poked her head out from a window on the second floor. She shouted some questions and disappeared. Soon afterwards, Zhijun's mother appeared at the window above. Xiaohui couldn't see her face clearly, but she was familiar with her hairstyle, posture and voice. She was almost the same as ten years before. She threw down the key, which had always been her customary act.

Zhijun's home looked like a warehouse. Except the furniture, all their possessions had been packed into cardboard boxes and each box was numbered. As a matter of fact, the whole building was packed with cardboard boxes. At the corner of the stairwell the briquette stove and the honey-comb briquette box were replaced by cardboard boxes, too. The door of every household was open and so were the doors and drawers of cabinets. The floors were covered with old newspapers and scraps of paper. This dilapidated house had reached its end and would be reduced to ruins. A high-rise building would stand here to signify the start of a new era. It would have nothing to do with the old residents. They would be driven away like birds scattering to find new nests after the old ones were destroyed. In those final days the dilapidated building was treasured and neighbors had never been on such good terms. The panic brought them together.

Xiaohui was not surprised to find Zhijun's mother playing mah-jong with the neighbors, dressed only in her pyjamas. They were sitting at a temporary table set up on a cardboard box. Walking from the ground floor to the third floor, she had already been enveloped by the atmosphere of reluctance towards parting. She felt relieved when she saw Zhijun's mother so happy there.

After finishing a round of the game, she stood up to greet Xiaohui. Her neighbors moved to another room to continue. It seemed that they were well prepared for this kind of disturbance. Xiaohui found those formerly nosey neighbors uninterested today. They didn't even look her in the face. Zhijun's mother stopped one old man and introduced him to Xiaohui, "This is Zhijun's father. He retired a few years ago and moved back to Shanghai."

Zhijun's father? She thought they had been divorced long before. Restraining her curiosity, she bowed respectfully to this dark-skinned old man. She regretted that she had not prepared a gift for him. Zhijun's mother said to the old man, "This is Xiaohui, Zhijun's good friend. Xiaohui," she emphasized her name, "went abroad and Zhijun has missed her."

Xiaohui found herself getting emotional. But through her tearful eyes, she could still see the light in his eyes and the warmth on his face. He wrung his hands in anxiety and mumbled, "I know,

I know. Zhijun often talked about her. What a pretty girl!" He looked at her from head to toe.

He searched the room and picked up an aluminium pan. He asked Xiaohui, "What would you like to eat? I'll go and get it for you."

Before Xiaohui declined, Zhijun's mother snatched the pan from his hands, saying, "How can you give Xiaohui food bought from the street vendor? Do you think she is a guest from your village? Go and serve her a cup of good tea. I'll cook something myself. You can go and play mah-jong afterwards. Don't stay here."

He brought the tea and was reluctant to leave. He started to say something, but was stopped by Zhijun's mother. She said, "Go away and let us have a chat."

Xiaohui asked from behind his back,

"How is Zhijun?"

He turned around slowly and explored Xiaohui with his eyes. He said, "Zhijun went to Japan and earned a lot of money. He said he could buy a house and get married as soon as Xiaohui came back ..."

"Heigh-ho, old man, that was a long time ago," Zhijun's mother cut him short. "If I had a pretty girl like her, I wouldn't let her get married in China. Besides, Zhijun can only afford a two-bedroom flat. Do you know what kind of house Xiaohui lives in? A villa! How can an ordinary flat be compared with that? Xiaohui, have you brought any photos with you? Show them to his father."

She shook her head. She felt so suffocated that she couldn't speak. She managed to conceal the upsurge of her emotions. Looking at the silent Xiaohui, Zhijun's father reluctantly walked out of the room.

In the past ten years Zhijun's mother had been ageing rapidly. The skin on her neck and hands was as flaccid as old rubber. Her extended youth had been defeated by time. Her facial features were still as beautiful as before though. Her bony face was as sexy as any urban beauty. If you removed the wrinkles, she was still a fashionable woman. Her never-changing hairstyle was the masterpiece of expert hairdressers. The old-fashioned hairstyle suited her age well. She knew that Zhijun's mother never washed her hair herself. Even during the Cultural Revolution, she had her hair done at the hairdresser's. Her resolute posture reminded people of her graceful figure in her youth. The way she slightly lifted her chin was a reflection of her unending self-confidence. She asked in an optimistic tone, "Do I look old? I've been ageing fast since his father returned. I don't know why a woman is ageing fast as soon as she lives a comfortable life. Take your friend Qinghua, for example. She became good-looking after her divorce. A woman will always look young while living a single life." She fixed her eyes on Xiaohui and shook her head, "Your face is getting thinner. Women are like this when they pass the age of 30. This is an indication of getting older. Of course, you're far from being really old. You look good. But your expression—how shall I put it?—sometimes it will betray you. You ... you don't smile as much as before. Does your husband treat you well?"

How come her marriage was written all over her face? Many people asked the same question. Maybe, a woman's happiness is decided by her marriage.

"He's much older than I am. On the whole, it's a happy marriage. By the standards of the Chinese Malaysians, we're a model couple." She tried her best to recount her real situation, but her words came out as a few half-hearted remarks.

Zhijun's mother lifted up her head and swung her short hair over her forehead. This was a habit she had formed during her dating days. The smile faded from her face.

"A mature man has a stable career and can support his wife. The question is whether he can satisfy her. Tell me the truth, Xiaohui, can he satisfy you?"

The question struck her like a thunderbolt. Qinghua would not ask such a question. Neither would Zhang Lin. Only Zhijun's mother would act like that. If she couldn't control the situation, things would be get out of hand. Though shocked, she forced her lips into a thin smile.

Zhijun's mother changed the topic of conversation as if she had not asked the question. She held out her arm and swept it over the furniture in the room. She said with a sigh, "We'll start moving the day after tomorrow. We'll live in a temporary home for two years. I have to store the whole set of mahogany furniture in three places." Her face clouded over and tears bathed her cheeks. "In order to protect this furniture from the rebels of his father's work unit, I threatened to cut my wrists. Xiaohui, I never gave up my dream. I waited for the day when I would move in to a house big enough to hold all the furniture. I risked my life safeguarding it. But what's the use? Our living space is getting smaller. The authorities will only give us a one-room flat. How can we squeeze the entire set of furniture in such a small flat?"

The existing room, an area of about twenty square meters, could hardly contain the whole set of furniture. It would be spread out in different locations. The day might not come when it was brought together again. In trying to look after the furniture, she would become a slave to it and be upset her whole life.

Xiaohui didn't know how to comfort her. You could only comfort a child. You couldn't comfort an adult, just as no one could comfort her for her life of regret.

The well loved furniture displayed its sumptuousness and timeless grandeur. But one day it would depart from the shabby old house. Many years ago, when she followed Zhijun and entered this room for the first time, she had this premonition. When she saw Zhijun's mother on her knees, cleaning the claw-like feet of the furniture so meticulously, she realized that this woman would risk her life for it. When she caressed the furniture with her fingers, Xiaohui could almost feel her pleasure. She sympathized with Zhijun's mother because women were sentimental about material things. However, they belonged to two different generations. Compared with long term happiness, a set of furniture was nothing. Xiaohui expected much more than this for herself. It was only natural that she felt as suffocated in Zhijun's home as in her own home. She was weighed down by the small-minded atmosphere in both. She knew that, passive as he was in nature, Zhijun would be swallowed up by this kind of life. Since he would not give it up, she had to let him go.

Zhijun's mother was well aware of this.

Even during the days when she and Zhijun were deeply attached to each other, his mother never bothered them with the subject of marriage. Being a woman of shrewd observation, she was generous and open-minded. As a mother, she had little maternal love. That's why she looked to reason when she judged the relationship between her son and his girlfriend. At the time she would joke with Xiaohui in the presence of her son, saying "When you marry a rich man, don't forget to give Zhijun a hand," or "I know Xiaohui will come back to see us, no matter how far away she goes. She is not sentimental, nor is she cold-hearted."

Zhijun didn't care about her remarks and said with a smile, "My mother will never grow up. She is full of imagination and likes to cook up stories."

But Xiaohui knew that was no imaginary story. She was applying for a visa to go abroad, but she would not tell Zhijun until she was successful. She didn't want to mislead him on purpose. She simply had a superstitious belief that the truth should be concealed until it was sure to succeed. Also, her going abroad was like fireworks. Once set off, the sparkles would attract great attention. What if she failed?

So far as her relationship with Zhijun

was concerned, she felt no compunctions at all, because their relationship was purely sexual. Zhijun once asked her, "If I keep courting you, will you marry me?"

She shook her head and gave him a decided answer, "No! Absolutely no! Where would we live? In your west side room? How? Use a cloth screen as a partition? Or build a wall?" She threw one question after another at him. With the true situation out in the open, the tender affection disappeared from her face. "Zhijun, how can we live such a life? I've shared the tiny room with my parents for over 20 years. If we're going to share a room with your parents after our marriage, when will I escape?"

"What if we have our own house?" Zhijun asked, unsure of himself.

"How is it possible?" she responded

flatly. "We're both nobodies in society. Who will give a house to us? Why would they?"

She didn't realize that she was wearing an icy expression on her face, making Zhijun think that she would leave at any minute. He immediately changed the topic of conversation and said with a smile, "So long as we're together for now, everything will be OK. I'll help you find a rich man in the future and you'll help me find a rich woman. We won't be worried about financial problems. We'll live a free and easy life. What do you think?"

That's what Zhijun was: a kind-hearted and simple-minded boy. How could she choose him as her lifelong companion? But for the time being they were compatible lovers, though she never admitted it at heart.

They met at the swimming pool. The long winter of swimming had left her full of vitality. As she began to get over Cheng Cong's departure, he faded from her mind. When spring started, a handsome boy was waiting for her outside the changing room of the swimming pool. They rode home together, pedalling against the strong wind of early spring. When the wind lulled, they free wheeled along the asphalt road. They smiled at each other. He couldn't help stretching his arm out and holding her shoulder. All this was very natural. She didn't turn down his advances because she was very attracted to him.

They were both fond of sports. He had a vigorous constitution and a child-like face. He was a year younger than her; in fact psychologically he was even younger. She felt free and easy with him, because Cheng Cong had been so overbearing.

They were constantly together, true companions. The swimming pool was the center of their world. There was no fitness center in Shanghai. Even if it had existed, they wouldn't have been able to afford it. When dance halls opened, they practiced there and turned into a pair of show offs later. But rising prices left them in difficult circumstances. When the tennis courts were open, they played a few times. They had to stop going because they couldn't afford the high prices.

When they couldn't find anywhere to kill time, they had to stay at home. At first she refused to go to his home, because she wanted to keep their relationship within certain limits. She often reminded him and herself that they were only playing with each other. Back then, she was determined to go abroad, but she had no specific destination. Her mother's eldest sister had lived abroad for many years. Some of the family were hoping for her help. In 1980 only a few people went abroad, but her friends and relatives were trying hard to achieve that aim. The departure of Cheng Cong was a great stimulus to her. Behind her father's back she persuaded her mother to ask her aunt for help. Around that time her father started to intervene in her relationship with Zhijun, complaining that Zhijun had no plans for his own future. In order to build a barrier between them, he set a deadline for her to come back home at night. As a result, Xiaohui asked for sick leave during the daytime and turned every day into a holiday.

During a rainy day they found no place to go. She was so bored that she agreed to go to Zhijun's home. This was a turning point for her. Ever since then she spent most of her spare time with Zhijun at his home. Such merry days! Had she been happy? She had only a hazy impression. She played games with Zhijun, sometimes with her whole heart, other times just superficially. While waiting to go abroad, she had to keep her distance. She couldn't commit herself to anything, because she was afraid that might lead to difficulties in the future. She didn't want to be responsible for that. The sun rose and set day by day. Time slipped by. The image of Cheng Cong flashed past her. She calculated that he ought to be a junior at university. She was anxious because she had staked everything on going abroad and still nothing was certain. During the lonely nights in Kuala Lumpur, she looked back on this period of time and felt that her cherished dream had been lost in the past. Trapped in depression and sadness, she would sleep walk into the garage. She drove at lightning speed through the dark as if she were driving back to the past. Later she would come back to herself. She would realize that Zhijun belonged to the past only.

Xiaohui presented a gift to Zhijun's mother, who smiled and wiped away her tears. She looked at the gold necklace with a gold Laughing Buddha pendant. She was especially taken with the pendant. Seeing her in a better mood, Xiaohui wanted to ask about Zhijun. His mother returned the gift to Xiaohui and said with a stern countenance, "I can't accept such a valuable gift. Zhijun will be angry!" Her refusal sounded harsh. Xiaohui felt embarrassed. "Why?" she let out, asking almost in a whisper, "does he hate me?"

Zhijun's mother heaved a sigh and said, "It was not right to separate the way you two did. Zhijun looked like a child but knew what was what. He seemed to grow up the minute you left him. He went to Japan to prove something to himself ..." She hesitated here and changed the topic. "What's the use of talking about all that? Xiaohui, let's forget about it. If I were you, I would have acted the same way. Zhijun was young and attractive. What other advantages did he have? If you had married him, neither of you would have been happy. He was unable to give you what you were longing for. I was watching closely. I tried to knock some sense into him from time to time and told him to give up on the idea."

After uttering these words, she became very quiet. Xiaohui couldn't learn anything from her about Zhijun or his address. After a few minutes of polite nothings, Xiaohui decided to go. She succeeded in persuading Zhijun's mother to accept the gift. It seemed to her that she was imposing something on Zhijun's mother and his mother was forced to accept it against her will. Xiaohui wanted to say good-bye to Zhijun's father. The mother summoned her husband from the back room. His father intended to say something to Xiaohui, but was silenced. He wanted to see her off, but Zhijun's mother stopped him.

Zhijun's mother saw her to the entrance of the alley. The nearby family was moving house. A big bulb was hung outside the wall and shining brightly on the forlorn scene. Most households had moved out and the empty buildings were as lifeless and ramshackle as worm-eaten hollow trees. The space illuminated by the electric bulb was dazzling. Against the background of dark buildings, the brilliant alley looked like a glass world where everything was surreal. The shadows of the people hurrying to and fro carrying things were just ordinary people. What they moved away was trifling and insignificant. What they couldn't move was indispensable and precious, closely linked to their lives ...

When they passed by the trash cans, they saw garbage overflowing. In the lamp light, it looked like a small second-hand stall containing tea tables, chairs, picture frames, table lamps, sofas, commodes, foot basins and chamber pots. An aged woman of over 70 stood by the garbage can and said, "What a sin! What a sin!" Two men threw away several bags of garbage including furniture, clothing and household utensils. An old rattan cradle was rocking in the heap of garbage. The old woman turned her mumble into a shout, "What a sin! What a sin!" The two men halted and one of them came back and said to the old woman in an apologetic tone, "Please take whatever you like. We're unwilling to throw these things away. But how can we move all the stuff we've collected over the years. They'll be thrown away anyway. We have to leave today, what can we do if we don't throw them away?" The man pointed to the house-moving truck and the last two sentences were addressed to the two onlookers—Zhijun's mother and Xiaohui.

"It's the same with our family. Even though we're unable to keep them, we're still reluctant to throw them away. So we've been throwing something away each day. That's the way we deceive ourselves. If you live in a place for 40 or 50 years and save one thing every year, you'll collect at least 40 or 50 things. We have a deep affection for those things, but others think they are worthless. Even second-hand shops won't buy them. Of course, it's difficult to find a secondhand shop nearby ..." Zhijun's mother held Xiaohui's hand and walked her to the entrance of the alley. She talked on and on baring her heart.

"I've got two camphorwood trunks of old clothes. Where will I dispose of them? Who wants those old-fashioned qipao dresses and mandarin jackets?

They are made of good satin and silk. How I hate to part with them! I was told that there was a stall on Nanchang Road purchasing old clothing. I put those old clothes in a cardboard box and told my husband to take it to the stall. Many people were there trying to sell their old clothes. When the stall owner saw so many clothes in a cardboard box, he offered a price at random without examining the clothes carefully. The offer was so low that it would have been easier to just throw them away. His father was reluctant to sell them and brought them back. So they are still with us. But we'll have to move the day after tomorrow ..."

"Just take them with you. They will make a good souvenir for your family," Xiaohui persuaded her in a soft voice.

"Even if we bring them with us, they

will be thrown away. The two camphorwood trunks must be sold. You can't even put a complete set of mahogany furniture in the one-room flat ..."

The mahogany furniture was always the focus of her worries.

She walked alone under the starlit sky. In order to enjoy it more, she strolled across the street to the front of the Shanghai Exhibition Hall. This section of sidewalk was as spacious as before. The spire typical of Russian imperial palaces stood out among a forest of modern high-rise buildings, displaying its majesty, uniqueness and fragility. This was the most romantic section of Nanjing Road. The mansion was surrounded by elegant, low-rise foreign houses. The former site of the Shanghai Commercial Mansion was a dense wood.

Though walled in, the green wood, together with the boundless sky, rolling clouds and flying birds left people high-spirited. In times gone by, she often left Zhijun's home at dusk. Leaving the alley, she would turn around and raise her head. More often than not, she would be dazzled by the rays of the setting sun around the pinnacle. If it happened to be a clear day (though clear days were seldom seen except in scorching summer), rosy clouds complemented the distant splendor of the classical structure. She would turn around and walk along a long wall. When she couldn't help turning back, she would find the rosy clouds disappear. The overcast sky would change her mood. During the rainy days, the mansion looked as unreal and lifeless as a stage backdrop. When she walked along the long wall, she was too depressed to turn her head.

She and Zhijun once went for a walk along the wall in the twilight. Feeling depressed and perplexed, they walked in silence for a long time. As the sun went down that night, she understood that life was unpredictable, and it was difficult to be master of one's own destiny.

The day before she left Shanghai, she and Zhijun went to the nearby café. She snatched an hour from her busy schedule to say good-bye to him. As she stole a look at her watch from time to time, they became increasingly sullen. When she got the three-month visa, Zhijun asked her, "You won't come back, will you?" She answered, "It's not that easy." But when Zhijun said, "People seldom talk about that country. If you are not used to the life there, come back to Shanghai

..." She cut him short, "It's not easy to go abroad. How can I come back again just like that?" She didn't want Zhijun to utter such remarks as "I'll wait for you." Just like her, Zhijun avoided the topic about her going abroad. It seemed as if the problem would not exist if he didn't mention it. However, six months before Cheng Cong went abroad, she discussed this problem with Cheng Cong again and again. If Cheng Cong had been in Shanghai, she might have decided not to leave. She hoped that she could hold on to her relationship with Zhijun until the day she left, but it was impossible. She was busy applying for the visa, buying clothes and saying good-bye to all her relatives and friends ... She was so busy that she wanted to make better use of her nights. At first Zhijun tried his best to help her, but later he didn't know how he could. She liked to do everything herself. They didn't see each other for almost two weeks before meeting in the cafe.

When they met again that day, she found a gap between them. She attributed this to the time when they'd been apart. Neither of them was in the mood to express sorrow over the parting. Actually, she had hoped she would avoid meeting him like this. Seeing her awkward and restless, Zhijun stood up and said, "I'll walk you home."

She said with a smile, "Your house is nearby. I'll walk you home."

He shook his head and heaved a sigh, "Why do you want me to go back home so early?"

She felt like crying and let him walk her home. They walked silently to tree-lined and deserted Gaolan Road. All of a sudden, he embraced her tightly, so tightly that it reminded her of their passionate days. But even then she couldn't share his sentimental feelings. She struggled out of his embrace. Instead, she put her arms round him from behind. Right then, the boy belonged to her. But she wanted to be rid of him. She walked him home.

When they returned to the long wall on Nanjing Road, they walked slowly and then stopped. They leaned against the wall and looked up. The strong wind was rushing through the wood and the treetops were cracking like whips. The howling of the winter was harsh, intimidating, but stirring. The land behind the wall would be covered by fallen leaves, making a sad and subtle scene. Zhijun's voice seemed to come from far away, "You're going to a tropical country. There's no winter there ..."

"Really? But I have a closet full of winter clothes!" She couldn't help laughing.

Zhijun laughed in reply. She said, "I like to see you in a jokey mood."

"Am I your personal entertainer?" Zhijun protested by tickling her.

She evaded him with a smile, saying, "What's wrong with an entertainer? I'll miss you when I am in a bad mood."

"It's a deal. Call me when you are in a bad mood. I'll get a phone line set up straight away," he said seriously.

She felt like crying. She toughened her heart and stopped a taxi.

"I've got to go. People are waiting for me at home. Let me know when you order the phone service." She ran toward the taxi.

When the car started to move, she

wound down the window and waved to him. With his hands in his pockets, he stood in front of the long wall, a lonely looking man. What a bleak scene!

Of course, they didn't call each other. Like many men and women, separation meant parting. The moment of parting escaped their memory. The scene of Zhijun standing in front of the long wall was like a shot in a second-rate sentimental movie. Were there any lyric episodes in her life? When she was young, she had a heart of stone. Without nostalgia or hesitation, she was determined to go after what she wanted.

Presently, Shanghai Center took the place of the former woods and open land. In the prime of spring, the atmosphere of summer was already prevalent. Some girls were wearing short-sleeved

T-shirts and mini-skirts. The long summer was yet to come. She was strangely worried about them. In spite of the fact that she had lived in a tropical country for ten years, she was impressed by the scorching summer here. She sat alone at the long bar on the second floor of the mansion. She ordered a glass of water only. With her chin held in both hands, she used one finger to stop a tear at the corner of her eye.

Chapter 4

Late at night she dialed Zhang Lin's number from her room in the hotel. As soon as she heard ringing tone, she was hesitant. She knew that the call would wake up Zhang Lin's husband and son. But she simply couldn't hold back. She had to talk to Zhang Lin. She wondered how she had got through those ten years when there was nobody she could speak her mind to. Zhang Lin immediately picked up the phone. She told her that they had just finished work for the day. After taking a bath, she was reading a newspaper on the bed. Zhang Lin sounded more at ease than she had before. She said jokingly, "My husband is still taking a bath. The best period of the day starts right now for him."

They had their own fun, though Zhang Lin didn't pay much attention to her appearance. Xiaohui kept silent.

"Xiaohui ..." Zhang Lin shouted, "I thought the line had been disconnected."

"I want to put back my return to Malaysia. I talked with my husband over the phone just now and he said he would not make a decision for me. But he just called to hurry me back. He wants me to negotiate a real estate deal ..."

"Oh, I don't think delaying is a good idea. The real estate deal must be big business. You can come back later. If having money, it's easy for you to fly back."

"It's easy to talk," she said impatiently. She was often touchy with Zhang Lin. "Business never stops. After you make a deal, you'll negotiate another deal. When you earn money this time, you want to earn more next time. I haven't come back in the past ten years because of unending business. I've thought the problem through, and I would rather sacrifice some money." She stopped suddenly. She didn't want to keep pouring out her constant complaints.

Zhang Lin didn't mind. She said calmly, "OK, since you're here, you should stay a few days longer. I was worried that I might not have time to talk with you. Renovation is under way and time is money ..."

"I'd like to go to Beijing," Xiaohui cut

in with determination, “to see Zhijun. Zhijun’s mother was quite resentful. I don’t want Zhijun to harbor any bad feelings about me. I made it clear to him that even if I didn’t get the visa, I would not marry him. That was absolutely true.”

“You’re going to Beijing just to tell him that? You must be out of your mind!” Zhang Lin scolded her. “So many years have passed. The scars are healed. Why do you want to bring it all up again? Did Zhijun wound you? You’re crazy!”

“It was you who urged me to see his mother.” Xiaohui was unreasonable with Zhang Lin just like 20 years before. “If his mother hadn’t mentioned it, how could I have got so upset?”

After a moment of silence, Zhang Lin said, “I regretted it after I told you. I thought you didn’t care much about

Zhijun. His mother has missed you in the past ten years. She is old and her son is not with her. The house moving has been getting to her. I thought you might be a comfort to her."

Xiaohui kept silent.

Zhang Lin asked confidentially, "What did she tell you?"

"Nothing serious. I knew she didn't say it on purpose. She has always been on my side," Xiaohui talked in a confused manner. "Zhijun is her son after all. She didn't blame me for that ..."

Zhang Lin listened closely.

"His mother said it was not right to separate the way we did ..." She was choked with sobs. "When I left, he was in good spirits. What ... what was in his mind, I ... I really had no idea ..."

"Anyway, many years have passed." Zhang Lin reminded her.

"I still remember it. How can he forget it?"

"Memories will fade. What's the use of talking about your past?"

She was not happy with Zhang Lin's sobriety. Zhang Lin always kept a cool head and expressed reservations about her love affairs with Cheng Cong and Zhijun. She was talking to the wrong person. She should speak to Qinghua. But she didn't have the nerve to call her. She always felt a little deterred by Qinghua. She remained speechless for a moment and then said with a sigh, "Forget about it. It's difficult to express myself. You could only understand this if you've been through it yourself. Please go to sleep. It's so late. I don't want to keep your family awake." She seemed to have just remembered Zhang Lin's family again. She hung up before Zhang Lin answered.

A few minutes later Zhang Lin called her back, "I've moved the phone to the room downstairs. They won't hear a sound. We can talk to our hearts' content, all night if you want."

That was Zhang Lin. She was a good person to know when you hit trouble. She recalled those days when she had a date with Zhijun. In order to avoid her father's opposition, she would ask Zhang Lin to come and fetch her. Usually Zhang Lin helped her mother prepare the supper when she got home from work. In order to play the role, she had to change into street clothes and go to Xiaohui's home. The round trip cost a lot of time, but she never complained.

When Xiaohui didn't answer, Zhang Lin went on, "Whether with Zhijun or with Cheng Cong, you must be clear about your motive. You've come back for a holiday. You don't have to involve yourself in emotional complications."

Xiaohui remained silent and Zhang Lin couldn't go on. They were silent for a few minutes.

"Help me get Zhuijun's address, will you? Yes or no? I only want a simple answer. Don't talk down to me. I'm over 30, and I know my own mind."

"I haven't kept his address. If you insist, I'll go to his home for it," Zhang Lin answered coldly.

A few instants later Xiaohui said in a low voice, "I haven't thrown a tantrum for years. To live there, I had to wear a mask."

"So you vent your spleen on me. But you ought to bare your heart to me ..."

"Do you offer me any time? You're so busy. I think I came back at the wrong time ..." Xiaohui lifted up her voice and felt embarrassed instantly. "Look, I'm complaining again!"

"I suppose you're entitled to be. It seems that pretty women can be brutal and unreasonable." Zhang Lin pretended to be serious. "When we were at school I always gave in to you, even though I got better marks. Do you know why? I worshipped you. I was ugly, I had to worship beautiful girls."

Xiaohui was moved by her distress. It was true that Zhang Lin had always been a good listener. It seemed that she had never had her own life.

"Do you know that I dare not sneeze in front of my husband?" She changed the topic, trying to make the conversation more light-hearted. "Before our marriage I once sneezed when I had a phone conversation with him late at night. He drove to my place at once thinking I was suffering from a severe flu ... He never sneezes himself because he considers it impolite. In order to match his good family upbringing, I've succeeded in controlling my sneezing ..." Before she finished the sentence, Zhang Lin sneezed violently. Both of them burst into laughter.

They hung up on good terms. With everything quiet, she still felt confused. Was it the result of her visit to Zhijun's home? She took up the bottle of sleeping pills on the nightstand and swallowed two pills. She knew a sound sleep would clear her thoughts.

She didn't go to bed immediately. Instead, she sat before the dressing table and observed her face in the mirror. She possessed a fine and smooth countenance, but a pale and thin face. Just as

Zhijun's mother mentioned, a woman's face began to thin after the age of 30. She used to have a rosy rounded face embedded with two brilliant big eyes. That kind of look was typical of beautiful women in the Tang dynasty. When she arrived in Kuala Lumpur, all the male relatives and friends of her aunt's family fastened their greedy eyes on her. That's why her aunt kept her under strict control and took her with her wherever she went. She had to guard against male intruders both inside and outside the family. Xiaohui became the common enemy of rich women. Her cousin—her aunt's daughter—got on well with her at first, but they later became estranged because her husband showered attention on Xiaohui. If she had not kept her aunt company and cheered her up, she would have been sent home by her aunt.

When she was young, she was not proud of her beauty. On the contrary, it became a burden on her. She was isolated from other students in high school. When she started to work at a factory after graduation, she was discriminated against because of it. She was assigned a job at the packaging workshop where only the old, feeble, sick, handicapped and retarded persons worked. Whether on campus, in the alley or at the factory, she was harassed by flippant men. At the time beauty was not respected in society. Though attractive, beautiful people and things were despised by some people. Her troubled feelings were soothed in 1978 when social order and regulations were changed. As soon as she got to Kuala Lumpur, she was relieved to live in the courteous upper class atmosphere of her aunt's social circle. With the lapse of time, she was aware of the fact that other women were on alert around her. So she always kept a low profile.

Even under her aunt's wing, she still managed to have a short love affair. He was a western diplomat, handsome and cheerful. They met at a party held at her aunt's house and fell in love with each other at first sight. Their secret love was like a melancholy and tender dream. Her visa would expire soon and he would leave his post abroad for home. They didn't speak the same language and communicated by using a few English words. She met him on her way to the post office or the pharmacy. Since time was short and she was afraid of being seen, every date was a memorable one. His car stopped at the crossroad near her aunt's home. As soon as she got in the car, he drove out of that section as fast as he could. Then he slowed down and held her hand with one of his. When the car stopped at the traffic light, he would turn round and embrace her. His enthusiastic kisses made her feel a feverish heat. In an instant she had to go back home and part with him. Just like getting out of a high-temperature room, she blushed hotly and was sweating all over.

This seemingly romantic love was not as pure and simple as Xiaohui had expected. She was racking her brains for a plan so that her lover working at the consulate might understand her predicament and help her. She was not a girl adept at scheming. She was reduced to despair because she lived a solitary life in a foreign country. Finally she worked out an absurd plan. She asked Qinghua, who had just graduated from university, to translate the letter she sent her and send back the translated version to her. All her trustworthy friends were in China. Her plan might be ridiculous, but it was sure to succeed. Qinghua spent two nights translating her letter into English (a very hard job for her because it wasn't her major), and sent the translated version back to her immediately. Xiaohui didn't expect the letter to take a month to return to her. When she received Qinghua's letter, her lover had been gone from Malaysia for five days.

She almost went mad with grief when she learned that he would leave. During their last date, he drove directly to his apartment regardless of her opposition. They made love for a couple of hours. She burst into tears at the end.

She didn't cry like this when Cheng Cong left her. Kneeling down naked on the carpet and covering her face with both hands, she begged him earnestly in Chinese, "Don't leave me alone here! Don't leave me ..."

He kissed every inch of her skin and mumbled in English, "I love you! I will come back! I will certainly come back!"

When he came back to Kuala Lumpur three years later, she was already engaged. When she received his call, she was drawing up an invitation list with her aunt. She didn't have any difficulty in communicating in English, but she declined his invitation. It was too late. She didn't want to take any risks. Her violent emotions had been suppressed long ago.

It was during those peaceful years

that she began to suffer from insomnia. She began to rely on sleeping pills. The following morning she would look pale. Even if she went to the fitness center, it didn't help her have those sound sleeps she had when she was young. Her face began to cave in. Though slimness was appreciated, nobody complimented her for her beauty.

She turned on the CD player she always kept with her. The bedroom was filled with sweet music. She got into bed and closed her eyes. After a while the sleeping pill would work and she would fall into a deep sleep.

She was woken up by the ringing. It was already 9 o'clock in the morning. Qinghua's loud voice meant that she was in high spirits.

"I know you're still sleeping because you belong to the decadent capitalist classes," Qinghua joked. "Are you available tonight? I want to take you out for Sichuan hot pot. Everyone eats it here in the winter. It's near the end of the season, but I'm sure it's still delicious. Zhang Lin will join us. I told her to have a facial, get a perm and put on a decent dress. Since this is our first get together for ten years, we have to do it right." Qinghua couldn't help laughing herself. Xiaohui was amused by her monologue, and her drowsiness disappeared immediately. She laughed too.

"Don't tell Zhen Zhen. She's shameless enough to come if she learns about it. I'm fed up with her. She is always bragging about her husband as if they are living a fairytale life." Qinghua was as sharp tongued as before. Xiaohui didn't join in because Zhen Zhen had been really nice to her this time.

"Qinghua, I want to make it clear that this will be my treat ..." She changed the topic of conversation but was cut short by Qinghua.

"There will be a lot of chances for you to treat us. It'll be on me tonight. Don't argue with me. I don't intend to pay for the meal. I'll try to get the money back."

While Qinghua was in high spirits, she would feel the same. That was the magic of Qinghua. She was far from being pretty. You couldn't even say she was good-looking. But she was always the focus of attention wherever she went.

Qinghua's grandfather was a priest in the Catholic Church. Her parents were medical specialists. Many people went to her home to seek spiritual or physical help. That's why Qinghua set herself apart from her contemporaries. She had great confidence of her maturity and liked to lecture others. As a result she gathered a group of worshippers round her. However, when she grew up, she had to go through tribulations in her life. She suffered a major setback in her affection for Cheng Cong. Her only rival in this love triangle was Xiaohui. But Xiaohui, who was drawn into the vortex, didn't know the truth until several years later.

She acknowledged Qinghua's superiority when they studied together. She was well aware that she had no advantage except her good look. She was average in academic study and had no other talents. Qinghua was a versatile student. She was top in all subjects except mathematics, which was Zhang Lin's strength. She also did well in extracurricular competitions, like recitation or painting contests. (Qinghua was good at painting picture posters.) At the same time Xiaohui came to realize that her isolation among the girl students was completely changed after Qinghua began to support her openly. Cheng Cong's secret help often produced negative results, because the handsome class monitor was the focus of attention for female students. His help was, in effect, intensifying girls' hostility towards Xiaohui. Eventually it was Qinghua who reminded him and helped him out of the predicament.

To other students, the relationship between the three was very strange. The talented Qinghua, who considered herself superior to others, was obedient to Cheng Cong, her co-monitor and intellectual inferior. While Cheng Cong formed an intimate relationship with Qinghua, he never concealed his concern for Xiaohui. Xiaohui accepted Qinghua's protection in spite of her condescending manner. Rumors about the three of them abounded throughout their school days.

After graduation, Cheng Cong volunteered to work on a farm in Anhui Province. Qinghua and Xiaohui were allowed to stay in Shanghai. All at once, their subtle relationship became clear-cut. The night before his departure, Cheng Cong came to say good-bye to Xiaohui. He asked, "Are you going to write to me?"

Xiaohui nodded her head, a little surprised by his serious manner. He asked, "Would you like to make our relationship different from our relations with others?"

Xiaohui became nervous and asked,

"What do you mean?" She was so muddled that she just blurted it out.

Cheng Cong hesitated.

"Xiaohui, didn't you … realise … I … always … liked you?"

"How can you …" Xiaohui turned round in shame.

They were at the entrance of her alley. Seeing her standing with her back toward him, Cheng Cong was worried, "Xiaohui, hey … people will think that I … Look, I won't talk about this anymore …"

As a matter of fact, Cheng Cong wrote down what he was going to say in his first letter to her. Once they started writing to each other, they established an entirely new relationship. It was the relationship Xiaohui had longed for but had not dared to go after. It seemed that she couldn't bear the intensity of her happiness. Seeing her face covered in smiles one day, Qinghua grew suspicious, "Xiaohui, you're much happier after graduation. Is Cheng Cong writing to you?"

"How ... how did you know?" Xiaohui smiled coyly, looking for an opportunity to reveal the secret.

"We've studied together for four years, and I know him too well." It sounded that Qinghua was talking about her most intimate friend. But at that time Xiaohui was not a good observer. Puzzled by Zhang Lin's stare of astonishment, Xiaohui asked Zhang Lin, "Do you think that's improper?"

Qinghua said, "Don't ask Zhang Lin. She's different from us. She religiously follows established routines. She will find a husband with the help of a marriage agency." She let out an ear-piercing laugh. Xiaohui still remembered how unpleasant it was.

Qinghua was eager to outdo others. Though devastated by the news, she never revealed her feelings in front of Xiaohui. Now that her doubts and worries of the past four years were finally confirmed, her self-respect was utterly destroyed. After their get-together, Qinghua asked Zhang Lin for a meeting that evening. Sitting on the lawn in the park, Qinghua burst into tears. She told Zhang Lin that her heart hurt as if her chest was being trampled ... It was not until Xiaohui parted with Cheng Cong and got a new boyfriend a couple of years later that she learned the truth.

Xiaohui was angry when she found out the truth and accused Qinghua of making a fool of her for several years. When she calmed down, she had mixed feelings. She knew her more honest moments with Qinghua started after her disappointment in love. Just as Zhang Lin said, painful experience brings people together. Anyway, they became close friends for a couple of years.

"As the tide of love recedes, a beach of friendship is left behind." Maxims like this were copied down in her diary when she was a high school student. She quoted this maxim when she wrote the first letter to Qinghua after she went to Malaysia. Qinghua answered in her letter, "Don't quote maxims all the time. These words are naïve and excessive. When will you be mature enough to describe your feelings with your own words?"

When she finally did, she had seen the world. No one wanted to listen when someone bared her heart. She tried several times to write to Qinghua, but changed her mind every time. She had a hundred things she wanted to share with Qinghua, but what good it would do? Eventually, she gave up on the idea.

Not long after she hung up, Qinghua phoned again. She said, "What a poor memory I have! I forgot to tell you the most important thing. That's always the case with me. I choose to talk about the less important thing first, to build up to something. But then I usually forget to get around to it."

"If your invitation to a dinner is less important, what else could be more important?" Xiaohui joked.

After a moment's silence, Qinghua shouted, "Xiaohui, you haven't wasted ten years. You're at least ten times cleverer than before. You're no longer what you were."

Xiaohui kept silent. Qinghua sensed something wrong and asked in a low voice, "Did I offend you?"

This was not Qinghua's usual tone. Xiaohui said with a smile, "Nothing. What you said reminded me of many things." Her tone was buoyant, "You still didn't tell me the most important thing."

"Actually it's nothing special," Qinghua had lost all interest. "I only wanted to give you a surprise. Maybe you won't be surprised. Who knows?" She became listless and tired.

"Why?" Xiaohui questioned her closely.

"Maybe to a sophisticated person like you, there is nothing surprising at all."

These words affected her. Qinghua could be the most intriguing person to talk to when she wanted to be.

Xiaohui pondered over what to wear for quite some time. Her clothes should not be too casual, or too elegant. In the company of plain women, Xiaohui always restrained herself subconsciously. She first chose a cream-colored linen costume. But she had to give it up because the costume came with a sleeveless top. During this season vests were all the rage in Shanghai. Male or female, old or young, everyone was wearing a long or short vest. The fashionable vests were so popular that they became unbearably vulgar. That was the way of things on the mainland. She recalled different periods of time when bell-bottoms, jeans and Teresa Teng's albums were the fashion of the day. When she came back, she noticed a great change in Shanghai. It was ironic that this habit still prevailed.

She finally selected a blue-white-pattern long skirt and a white close-fitting short blouse. She wore no jewels except a platinum ring. Like many women, Xiaohui was obsessed with her wardrobe. She was even choosey about nightgowns. There was an old saying, "A woman is well dressed for her admirer." Whom would she be well dressed for? After she made herself up, Zhen Zhen came to her home. She looked her over quickly and said, "Since you're on your way out at this time, you're going to a dinner, aren't you?"

Xiaohui forced an awkward smile. She felt sorry that she couldn't tell Zhen Zhen the truth, as she'd promised Qinghua. But Zhen Zhen didn't mind at all. She said, "I've come to see your father. He asked me to recommend a good cardiologist for your mother ..."

When Zhen Zhen mentioned her mother's illness, Xiaohui became upset. After she came back to Shanghai, she spent less and less time visiting her mother in the hospital. She had promised to keep her mother company for the whole evening, but Qinghua's invitation changed her plan. She paid her mother a short visit and had to leave the hospital. Her mother complained, "You won't stay long in Shanghai this time, but you still begrudge me your precious time!" With the lapse of time, her mother became more and more attached to her. She had no other children. She looked upon her future as an abyss which she dared not look into. She had never discussed her future with her husband, because this was a taboo subject for them. She tried her best to prevent her thoughts from wandering, but she felt irritable and restless.

"My father is too much! Why didn't he go directly to Qinghua, since her father is the head of the hospital?"

Zhen Zhen giggled, "No wonder your father didn't consult you. Your information is out of date. Her father retired long ago but was re-employed for a couple of years. He had a stroke before he got to be an outpatient specialist. As for her mother, she has such a fiery temper that she doesn't get along with people. What's more, she doesn't work in that section and she has to ask somebody else for a favor. I'll tell you what, nowadays the most popular are the middle-aged doctors who have returned from abroad ..."

Xiaohui knew Zhen Zhen's father was an administrator in the public health bureau and he had reached the age of retirement. Zhen Zhen read her mind and explained, "I didn't use my father's connections. My husband can deal with it. Who doesn't want to curry favor with a powerful man? He has plenty of connections."

She was bragging about her husband again! To Xiaohui though, her remarks were not as nauseating as Qinghua would have found them. She was just passing through. Why should she bear a grudge against her?

Zhen Zhen had hardly finished her words before she touched Xiaohui's clothes to feel the quality of the material. She asked, "Did you buy this here?"

"No, I bought it in Hong Kong. I like shopping in Hong Kong. The quality is good and you don't have to pay a fortune."

Zhen Zhen narrowed her mouth to show disapproval, “I’m not sure about these clothes. The clothing sold at the franchise store on Huaihai Road is much better. Of course, the price is astronomical. But, it’s nothing to rich people. A woman as rich as you are doesn’t need to buy cheap goods.”

“It has nothing to do with cheap goods. I mean the same clothing is sold cheaper in Hong Kong,” Xiaohui explained, trying to conceal her annoyance. “Anyway, clothing should be judged by its appropriateness, not by its price.”

“If you walk on the street in this kind of clothing, nobody will think you’re from abroad. Are you dressing down on purpose? Actually, it doesn’t matter. People in Shanghai are open-minded and they’ll wear anything fancy.”

Xiaohui gave a thin smile in reply. She ought to have told Zhen Zhen: high-class clothes are never fancy. Their uniqueness is displayed in the plain design. However, a cocksure person like Zhen Zhen would only ever know about her immediate surroundings. For example, she noticed Zhen Zhen was wearing an elegant knit suit. The whitish blue color was too light and the soft material revealed her podgy stomach. Though expensive, the suit didn't do anything for Zhen Zhen. She was not in a position to be openly critical, nor was she willing to shower praises. So she kept silent toward Zhen Zhen's new suit. Zhen Zhen thought Xiaohui looked down upon her, so she had become indignant.

In order to comfort Zhen Zhen, Xiaohui said, "I've seen a lot of rich people in the mainland. All the famous brands are in the shops. Even in the developed countries, not many people buy high-class goods like those."

"That's true. My husband went to Singapore on business and brought me some cosmetics. The local office worker acting as his guide told him that people in the office never bought luxury goods." Zhen Zhen was pleased with herself.

Xiaohui nodded her head.

"I found the Jinjiang Dixon Center across Jinjiang Hotel was the copy of a commercial street in Paris. Both of them sell almost the same brands ..."

"You've been to Paris?" asked Zhen Zhen, who felt disheartened.

"What other countries have you been to?" Zhen Zhen asked anxiously.

A faint smile crept across Xiaohui's face. She said, "A dozen countries. I went there on business. I was not in the mood for pleasure. Some places almost made no impression on me. I found those trips totally uninteresting."

Zhen Zhen nodded her head with emotion, "Although you live in a small country, you're free to go anywhere. Foreigners are different from us Chinese."

Seeing Zhen Zhen in low spirits, Xiaohui felt out of sorts, too. After a moment's silence, she said, "No matter where you live, everything depends on your attitude. You're satisfied with your husband, and I really admire you for that."

A light of joy radiated from Zhen Zhen's eyes. She looked at Xiaohui with certain intensity, sensing a touch of regret in Xiaohui's remarks. That's what she was after. She was looking for some flaws in Xiaohui's success. She was always eager to outshine others. She needed this to maintain her dignity.

"It almost sounds like you're not satisfied with your husband. I'm only kidding ..." Zhen Zhen smiled to herself. "You've never talked about him. I haven't seen his picture. I have no impressions of him at all. I feel as if you're still single ..."

Xiaohui became grim-faced. Zhen Zhen's heart was throbbing with excitement because she had touched her weak spot. Xiaohui almost lost her composure. Zhen Zhen stopped before going too far and said good-bye to Xiaohui.

"Please rest assured, Xiaohui, I'll take care of your mother's request. Since we're neighbors for decades, I'd help her even if we'd never been classmates." Zhen Zhen regarded herself as a kind woman and gave a lenient smile.

"Zhen Zhen, I think if we pay more, the hospital will provide better doctors. Don't bother using your connections; you might end up owing too many favors." Xiaohui knitted her brows slightly.

"The problem is you can't just look at a price list. Even if you are willing to pay, you still need to have the right connections." A complacent smile passed over Zhen Zhen's face.

Xiaohui produced a thick wad of money from her handbag and handed it to Zhen Zhen. She said, "Please take the money and spend it giving gifts and taking a taxi. When everything is settled, I'll give you more."

The smile faded from Zhen Zhen's face. She stormed to the door and said in a scornful tone, "Hey, Xiaohui, don't forget you're in China. Here people value friendship above anything else. My husband has two company-owned cars at his service. We could open a gift shop with the presents he's received. All our socializing gets refunded. Money is almost worthless in a family like ours." As soon as she uttered these words, she hurried out of the door. Xiaohui didn't stop her.

At dusk the street was jammed with a long train of cars. Xiaohui had to rush to the hotel decided by Qinghua.

Jostling through the crowd was a common scene on a Shanghai street. Sometimes, when she was down, she enjoyed the feeling of rubbing elbows with others. But now this kind of familiarity seemed very strange to her. It was not easy to walk quickly in the crowded street because you had to avoid people rushing the other way. She considered it a kind of exercise. Her body was rejuvenated in the workout and her heart was cleansed like the sky after the clouds had dispersed. Zhen Zhen had delayed her and affected her good mood. However, she saw this as a minor episode and dismissed it from her mind. What lay ahead of her was the gathering she had been looking forward to for ten years.

Chapter 5

In addition to plenty of delicious food, Qinghua ordered the waiter around in an impressive manner. Zhang Lin's upswept fringe looked like a flag flying in front of her forehead. Holding chopsticks, Xiaohui stared at them with a sunny smile. Just as she had imagined, the three of them got together in a cozy restaurant. While feasting, they were lost in a sweet sea of memories.

The waiter filled their glasses with beer. Qinghua and Xiaohui raised their glasses at once.

"What shall we drink to?" Qinghua glanced at Xiaohui and Zhang Lin in turn with a strange smile.

"First of all, let's drink to Xiaohui's return as a successful career woman!" Zhang Lin spat out a shrimp shell, mumbling.

Qinghua frowned, saying, "A bit cliché ..."

She tried again, "Well, we've lived through ten years and we finally have the chance to eat together, here's hoping for many more of these occasions while we're all still around." With these words Zhang Lin picked up a paper napkin and cleaned her sauce-dripping fingers. She held up the glass and with a shake of her hand the beer spilled on the sizzling sauté beef.

Qinghua flashed a serious smile at

Zhang Lin. "You spoiled a good dish to get your way."

Xiaohui couldn't help laughing.

Suddenly her laughter turned into tears.

All three became silent. Then Qinghua said, "What's the matter with you? Don't be so sentimental. At our age and with your life experience, you ought to be more restrained."

As tears were streaming down her cheeks, Xiaohui buried her head in her arms.

Zhang Lin didn't utter a word and went on eating the shrimp. Qinghua became anxious, "Zhang Lin, why don't you say something? Somebody will join us in a minute, and Xiaohui will lose face if her eyes are swollen."

"Who else did you invite? You told me it was just the three of us, didn't you?" Zhang Lin was irritated.

Qinghua ignored her and turned over to pat Xiaohui on the shoulder, "Cheng Cong will be here within half an hour. He was invited to two dinners this evening, the first one on business, and the second one ..."

Xiaohui got up and took hold of her bag. She was about to leave when Qinghua stopped her, saying with a sneer, "I gave this dinner in your honour. How can you be so inconsiderate?"

"It's not right to force other people into accepting your 'good intentions.' You decided for yourself to invite Cheng Cong to join us without asking Xiaohui whether she wanted to see him ..." said Zhang Lin.

Qinghua was so angry that she threw the cigarette lighter onto the table. She took out a cigarette and lit it.

Xiaohui raised a glass of beer and clinked it against Qinghua's glass. She gulped down the whole glassful. Without even wiping the foam off her lips she spoke, "I'm grateful to you, Qinghua," she glanced at Zhang Lin, "but I'm not mentally prepared to meet him right now ..."

"It's not that serious. It's only dinner." Qinghua said, "Men are not as serious as women. He came to Shanghai yesterday. When he learned that we would meet, he insisted on coming. Anyway, Xiaohui always keeps herself together, especially in front of a man. That's why I made arrangements on my own." She addressed the last two sentences to Zhang Lin.

Cheng Cong showed signs of becoming fat, though he was not considered a fat man. "You must have gained 20 pounds in weight, or maybe more?" she asked him as soon as they met. The 13-year-long separation and the difficult emotions of her youth were negated by this observation. The three of them burst into laughter—Qinghua, Zhang Lin and herself.

"How could you greet him like this?" said Zhang Lin.

"It demonstrates how important weight is in Xiaohui's life," said Qinghua.

"That's true. I weigh myself every day," said Xiaohui.

The three women talked with each other and Cheng Cong smiled at them. Though he wore a Western-style suit and well-groomed hair, Cheng Cong was no longer a focus of attention for the young girls on the street.

"I seldom see American people wear suits." She said in a regretful tone, glancing at him. At the same time, she took some food with her chopsticks.

"I'm just dressed the way Chinese people expect now. They judge you on these kinds of things," he apologized.

As soon as their eyes met, they dropped them again.

Xiaohui started to eat. She felt hungry. It was strange that she was hungry. She remembered how she began to enjoy swimming after Cheng Cong left. With wild enthusiasm she danced in the water. Every time she got out, people sitting at the side of the pool fixed their eyes on her. Only then did she realize the importance of keeping up her beautiful appearance. After swimming she always felt hungry. When she saw a big casserole of braised pork cooked by her mother, she would eat three bowls of rice mixed with the gravy. The pleasure of food was consolation for her disappointment over Cheng Cong. Afterward she often regretted her untimely pangs of hunger. Was her biological clock irregular?

What an appetizing dinner! Only in China did she have the chance to enjoy so many excellent dishes at a meal. She noticed Qinghua had ordered a number of her favorite dishes such as cuttlefish, mashed beans with salted vegetables and yellow mud snail. While eating these delicacies, she thought of her favorite soaked rice. It would go well with the dishes. She asked the waiter to bring in the rice. When she asked the other three whether they wanted some, all of them shook their heads. They were puzzled to see her pour her tea over the rice. When they saw her relishing it, they couldn't help laughing. Zhang Lin said in a low voice, "Those dishes are enough to fill you up. What's the use of eating rice, especially tea-soaked rice?"

"You don't get it. This is called 'recovering her original purity and simplicity;' everyone's doing it." Qinghua assumed her customary sarcastic tone.

"It seems we're following fashions unintentionally, because in my house we eat soaked rice every day," Zhang Lin blurted out.

Xiaohui covered her mouth to conceal her amusement as Cheng Cong caught her eye with a knowing smile. Qinghua observed them with her penetrating eyes. Acting as if there was nobody around her, she carefully spat out the shell of the yellow mud snail and left the dark mud on her lips.

After dinner Cheng Cong took the bill from Qinghua's hand and paid it in his direct manner. Men always paid bills for women in this way. It made Cheng Cong look fascinating. The three women were gazing at him, as if in a trance.

She suddenly discovered that Cheng Cong's hands were as delicate and slender as those of her husband. Both of them had soft and delicate hands that were quite feminine. Before their marriage, her heart was throbbing when she held his hand by accident. She was not able to define her own feeling ... After marriage her husband took the doctor's advice and slept separately from her because of his chronic disease. Later they didn't touch each other's hands at all. She didn't want to touch his hand because she detested him physically. She turned her eyes away from Cheng Cong's hands. Those associations were both unpleasant and unreasonable. However, her heart seemed to have been run over by a garbage truck, leaving a nasty stench in its wake.

Seeing Xiaohui anxious and distracted, Zhang Lin urged Qinghua to go with her. "Let's go. If we stay here, they'll think we're playing gooseberry."

Qinghua's face clouded. She stared at Cheng Cong with deep emotion. Even far away Xiaohui noticed Qinghua's unusual stare. With a puzzled look, Xiaohui moved her eyes from Qinghua to Cheng Cong. Cheng Cong nodded and gave a brief smile to Qinghua. "We'll stay for a while and I'll call you when I go back to the hotel," she said.

Qinghua followed Zhang Lin and left the restaurant. Cheng Cong said to Xiaohui, "She is helping me with a transaction."

They moved to the bar in the hotel lounge. The candlelight flickered across their faces. The spacious lounge was decorated with ornamental plants. Her heart throbbed when she noticed his warm stare.

When they were in love, they wrote to each other, revealing their feelings. When they expressed their beautiful and drifting mood, they never used the word "love." After exchanging letters for three years, he passed the university entrance examination—resumed after the Cultural Revolution—and came back to Shanghai from the farm in Anhui. One year later he went to the States. He spent most of the year in the university library. She learned afterward that he had been learning English vigorously, but at the same time he was undecided about going to America. Their love was a love of the mind; there was never any physical contact. Maybe a union like that was more open and its reverberations reached much deeper. As a result, she was spared the profound agonies of despair when he left. She had preserved a vivid memory of the days spent with him and regarded him as a background to those unforgettable years. While sitting face to face with him now, she felt estranged from him. The things that brought them together had drifted away with the passing of their youth. It took time to find a new basis for conversation. His position in her heart had never been replaced by somebody else, so she found it difficult to talk with him as an ordinary old acquaintance.

Seeing her remain silent, he stopped talking himself. Though he wanted to share his feelings with her, he was unwilling to initiate the conversation. He found her as beautiful as before, or even more beautiful than before. But just like a flower coming into full bloom, she was starting to lose the tenderness of youth. The love of this kind of woman usually ended in tragedy. That's why she sat there in an arrogant and unapproachable manner like a beautiful but cold statue.

He was not sure of his relationship with her. When she was a girl in early maturity and full of vitality, he could only convey his emotion from a distance. He didn't have the courage to reveal his heart to her. He had looked on his desire for her as a crime. During those years his sensual desire was like a chorus reverberating throughout his body. He concealed his desire tightly and cultivated himself as a model youth, advocated by society and an idol for the young girls around him ... When he arrived in America, he realized how stupid he'd been. But there was no time for regret. He had to face another harsh reality. During the years that followed, in order to make up for the sexual hunger of his youth, he became as uninhibited as western people. He was so given to debauchery that he lost all feelings of pleasure. It was a long period of indulgence that was never able to satisfy him. As the sexual ideal of his youth, Xiaohui would always remain distant and unapproachable.

The most vital part of his body was now useless. Her eyes flashed with memories of the past. They started to talk but kept their distance and stuck to trivialities. Both of them felt the gulf between them though they sat so near.

She felt exhausted by the indifference of her meeting with Cheng Cong. As soon as she came back to the hotel, she took a shower and jumped into bed. Woke up from a dream by the phone, she picked up the phone in a daze, not knowing where she was.

There was no sound on the other end. She was too startled to sleep anymore. She turned on the light and asked who was calling. Then came Zhang Lin's soft voice, "Xiaohui ... how are you?" She talked with a heavy heart.

"What's the matter with you? What happened?" Xiaohui asked in a loud voice. She put out her tongue. She found her voice had become much louder after she came back to China.

"I was worried about you. Now I'm relieved. You sound OK." Zhang Lin assumed her natural tone, "He, Cheng

Cong ... was he nice to you?"

"Oh, so that's what you were worried about ..." Xiaohui lowered her voice. She was obviously downhearted. After a moment of silence she raised her voice again, "So many years has passed. Maybe I have a poor memory. Anyway he seemed a stranger to me. Though sitting face to face with him, there was no chemistry between us. I don't know why." She continued, "It takes time to get familiar again. The relationship between us is in the past ... Zhang Lin, we didn't stay longer than an hour. He had another appointment ... I noticed he and Qinghua are on good terms?"

Zhang Lin heaved a sigh. She was frustrated, too.

"I didn't notice it until tonight ... I don't know Qinghua's intentions. It was she who arranged your meeting with Cheng Cong. But ..." Zhang Lin couldn't find appropriate words to describe Qinghua's stare at Cheng Cong. "She is clever, but sometimes she does dumb things."

Xiaohui kept silent. Zhang Lin said, "Xiaohui, Qinghua didn't tell me everything ..."

Xiaohui cut her short, saying, "Zhang Lin, you don't have to explain anything." Xiaohui was not as engrossed as Zhang Lin. She said with a yawn, "I'm dead tired today ..."

"On my way back home, I came across Zhijun's mother and got his address from her. Please take a pen and jot it down ... Hello, Xiaohui, are you there?"

"I was thinking whether it was worth recreating the past."

Zhang Lin ignored her and read

aloud Zhijun's address. There was a pen on the nightstand and a business card underneath. This was Cheng Cong's card. Xiaohui wrote down Zhijun's address on the back of the card.

Xiaohui had hardly hung up when the phone rang again. It was Qinghua's voice.

"I dialled several times, but it was busy."

"Zhang Lin called."

"I thought so. What were you talking about? You must have been gossiping about me. No wonder my ears are hot."

"Your plan worked. We were talking about you, about your good relationship with Cheng Cong," Xiaohui blurted out without thinking. In order to cover up her jealousy, she added, "You were on good terms in high school. You were both monitors."

"Not the same! Our relationship in high school was an illusion. It's something real now," she said, challenging Xiaohui.

They both fell silent for a moment. Then Qinghua said, "I knew you'd read the signs at the restaurant. I want to give you an explanation. I'll tell you what ..." Qinghua said sternly, "You know he often came back to China over the past three years. He liked to talk with me every time he came back. It's true that he sees me as his only intimate friend in the world."

"Why did you arrange a meeting between him and me?"

"For you, and especially for him. You both wanted it. I'm willing to do anything to see him happy."

"Is this what you really want to tell me?" Xiaohui said in a gloomy mood.

"No. This is only a prelude. I want to tell you the difference between his relationship with me and with you. It isn't a sexual relationship."

"Neither was mine!" Xiaohui shouted indignantly.

"It didn't happen, but it was always in the air. He had fantasies about you at any rate. Xiaohui, you were the sexiest woman in the world to him. As for me, he-he ..." She seemed to be smiling. "I'm only his friend, a sexless friend. He's unable to offer me anything more. Three years ago something went wrong with him in that department."

Bang! She felt blood surging into her head. In a daze she sensed Qinghua's voice fading away in the distance. She asked herself, was this the curse of fate? While living a long sexless life with her husband, she had fantasies about her liaison with Cheng Cong.

"Xiaohui, are you there?" Qinghua's question interrupted her train of thought. She heard Qinghua saying, "That was the result of his unbridled behaviour. He told me he was given to debauchery because his desire was suppressed during his youth. It had something to do with you ... Of course he will never reveal the truth to you. Like many people, he puts on a show in front of his most beloved ..."

"Then why did you tell me?" Xiaohui asked, feeling a surge of resentment.

"We're both women. At the crucial moment I'll stand on the side of a woman." Her tone of self-ridicule was replaced by a sudden sincerity. "When they pursue their illusory dreams, women often destroy something valuable that they already possess. Did you think I was ignorant of the fact that you had feelings for him? Now is the time for you to forget him."

After she hung up the phone, she went to the bar downstairs and drank a glass of wine. She wasn't a heavy drinker. She never smoked. She wouldn't even consider drugs. Temperance was her code of conduct. She would never do anything that could affect her looks or health. A glass of wine would help her sleep. This was the treatment she adopted when she lost confidence in sleeping pills. If she were in Kuala Lumpur, she would speed on the expressway. When she held the steering wheel, her hands would never shake. Wasn't she just going to drive off the road one day? She stopped her train of thought, just as she was afraid to look out of the window at the top of a high-rise.

She woke up at midnight. She had

slept for only four hours. Just like sleeping pills, wine gradually had less effect on her. Any medication will gradually lose its potency. What else could help her sleep? She got up and opened the window. The dew-moistened air covered her naked skin like a fine rain. It was during the wettest hours before dawn that her only desire came to her: she was going to see Zhijun.

The clear and vast sky was scattered with silvery stars. Then the first rays of the dawning sun spread like a veil and the fading stars started to disappear behind it. The morning sky glowed lustrous colors. The round full sun finally emerged above the roofs and was shining with boundless brilliance. It was a fine morning and she would go through the formalities to postpone her journey back to Malaysia and take the earliest available flight to Beijing. Seeing Zhijun might be the most joyful moment of her trip home.

Her decision had left her full of vitality. She put on jeans and sneakers and jogged along the bicycle lane. She was ushering in a more productive morning than she imagined. She had a big western breakfast at the hotel restaurant. She made phone calls in the hotel room, packed her luggage and went to the airline office.

Once she was seated in the first-class cabin, the exhaustion hit her. It was the period before noon, the most promising time of the day. The more influential companies and shops on the bustling streets started business at this hour. However, Xiaohui closed her eyes and fell asleep as the plane roared into the sky.

Chapter 6

She tried to call Zhijun at Beijing airport. When she picked up the phone, she shuddered at the thought of Zhijun not being at home. What would she say if somebody else answered the phone, his wife for example ...? But the phone was already ringing; there was no going back. She heard Zhijun's voice, a clear voice still familiar to her. Her heart was thumping. She had never experienced this during the three years she was dating him.

"It's me, Zhijun!" She blushed as if they had enjoyed some kind of playful intimacy the day before.

There followed a silence. Finally Zhijun answered, "Xiaohui, where are you?"

"I've just arrived at Beijing. I'm on my way to see you. I've come here for the sole purpose of meeting you," she said in her impulsive fashion. She was used to ordering him about.

There was another prolonged silence. She hadn't expected his hesitation. Then Zhijun said, "I'm going to the hospital because my wife is ill ... seriously ill. I've been staying with her in the hospital, and I just came home to fetch something."

It was Xiaohui's turn to be silent. A moment later she said, "I'm sorry, Zhijun. I had no idea. What's she suffering from?"

"Myocarditis. She had an attack before. She has congenital heart disease, so it's especially dangerous ..."

"Can I do anything for you, Zhijun? Do you need ... need ... money?" she asked with difficulty. She really wanted to help him, but she didn't know how to express herself.

Zhijun seemed to read her mind and laughed a little, "Money is not all that crucial. Her father is a high-ranking official. Her two brothers own a big company, and we're shareholders. Actually, we ... we've made a fortune." His voice was fading. In her mind he appeared small against the background of his wife's distinguished family. Zhijun said with a sigh, "She's in a first-class hospital in Beijing. But with her disease, doctors have limited options ..."

She nodded her head knowingly. It appeared to be a disease, but in reality it was a predestined misfortune. Who could avoid setbacks forever? Poor Zhijun, he was no longer a carefree boy. How much she wanted to console him!

"Zhijun, I'll visit her at the hospital in the afternoon,and we can meet there." Xiaohui made the decision without soliciting Zhijun's opinion. She suddenly realized that she was always full of herself with Zhijun. She sighed in a tender manner, "Zhijun, I've come to Beijing just for you."

Zhijun couldn't turn down Xiaohui, although he had made up his mind to forget her completely. When she went abroad, he was badly hurt by her departure. He recalled with longing the physical pleasures he experienced with her. He came to realize that the three youthful years spent together with Xiaohui were given in place of his future happiness. He felt as if he lost everything to her. How could she stay away for ten years without thinking of him? His pride was hurt, but he didn't hate her. He was not the kind of man who could hate a woman. To appreciate the true delights of life he needed a female's subtle guidance.

When he heard Xiaohui's voice again and her tender demands, he was too excited to contain himself. Though he was aware that it was inappropriate of her, he quickly gave in. He would do anything for her.

After he hung up, he was almost beside himself. How could he face Xiaohui calmly in front of his wife? At the same moment, a wave of passion surged through Xiaohui's body. Intimate details from the past came back to her. She felt the blood pulsing through her veins. She was astonished by the difference between her urgent desire for Zhijun and her nervousness before she saw Cheng Cong. It might be that her pure sexual desire for Zhijun didn't leave space for anything else.

She went to the hospital ten minutes early. Before the taxi driver stopped the car, she saw Zhijun standing near the door. He had always arrived early for a date with her. He looked relaxed while he was waiting. He kept facing straight ahead and didn't glance around, childish but persevering. He dressed the same way: T-shirt, jeans and sneakers. Even the way he carried himself was as smooth and powerful as when he was young. She was elated to see her familiar Zhijun as if her dream had come true.

With her tear-stained smiling face hidden behind a big bunch of flowers, she walked toward him quietly. He turned his head and saw her. He fastened his eyes on her and asked a nonsensical question, "Did you come by taxi?"

She didn't answer. She just stared at him with a smile. The dark shadow of his stubble added to his virile appearance. Men like him became more attractive as they got older. She fixed her eyes on him for a while and saw signs of his maturity. She caught sight of the faint wrinkles around his eyes and mouth. The passing of the years was deeply etched on his face.

The hospital was more luxurious and imposing than she had expected. His wife's ward was on the highest floor of the building. As the elevator moved upwards, it gradually emptied. At last she and Zhijun were left alone. As soon as the door closed, Zhijun took hold of her hand, and tears welled up in his eyes.

She turned her head to evade his eyes. She was too weak to pull her hand away. She mumbled, "Don't ... Zhijun. I'm going to see her in a minute ..." The elevator door opened before she finished speaking. There they had arrived.

Zhijun's wife Yanyan didn't look feeble or emaciated. On the contrary, she was still plump and smooth-skinned. Maybe it was the result of being bedridden so long. Only her pale face and greenish-purple lips indicated her illness. Her regular features and good figure gave her a hardy attractiveness—a contrast to her illness.

She pronounced Xiaohui's name as if it was familiar to her from conversations with her husband. Xiaohui gave the flowers to her and saw the nightstand was already covered with many bunches. She said, "I've been away for years and lost contact with many old friends. I've tried my best to see as many of them as possible. I've come to Beijing on business, and I wanted to see Zhijun. I learned from him that you're ill ..." A seemingly justifiable explanation of the reality helped to cover up the deceptive intention beneath it.

Yanyan didn't pay any attention to her remarks. She smelled and kissed the bunch of flowers in her arms.

"I cannot love flowers enough. I'm longing to die among piles of flowers." Her remark sounded as if she was playing the pampered child or she was making threats.

Xiaohui gave a troubled glance to Zhijun. She was always at a loss responding to small dramas like this. Zhijun took the basin and went out of the ward as if he hadn't heard anything. Yanyan said with her head buried among the flowers, "I knew you would come back, come back to see Zhijun." It was her response to Xiaohui's previous words. "I waited and waited for years. Several times I was on the brink of death, but I thought it would be a shame that I had not seen you ..."

"I love Zhijun, but in the past few years I haven't really possessed him, just as he hasn't really possessed you. It's an unjust fate!" She was biting her finger bitterly. "That's why I like to be ill. I like to see Zhijun busy attending me all day long. I have a sense of security when I'm ill." She had a smug smile on her face just like a child who succeeded in teasing an adult.

As soon as Zhijun came back from the bathroom, Xiaohui took her leave and said to Yanyan, "I'll leave China pretty soon. Take care of yourself. I can see he cares a lot for you. Your full recovery will be his best reward, don't you think?"

Yanyan didn't answer her question directly. She said, "What a man wants most is something he is never able to get."

Xiaohui didn't want to prolong the conversation. She picked up her handbag and said good-bye to Yanyan. Yanyan said in a loud voice, "Wait a minute. Promise me you'll have a meal together with Zhijun. You need to have a good talk with each other. Since you haven't seen each other for a long time, he will invite you on my behalf." Then she said to Zhijun, "Try to go to the best restaurant nearby. It's busy from five to seven. You may as well stay out for a couple of hours."

Xiaohui was caught off guard again. She was speechless. It was not until she walked out of the ward that she woke up all of a sudden and said to Zhijun, "You'd better go back. She, she scared me. I don't want to eat, especially at a time like this."

"Don't take to heart what she said. If you don't want to eat, we can find a place to talk, since she's granted me two hours' leave," said Zhijun.

They went to a small restaurant. As there were no other customers, it was quiet. The passion that flared up in the elevator had gone away. With Yanyan's shadow between them, she felt agitated. It was a bad choice to have a date near the hospital. The smell of disinfectant and death seemed to linger. Yanyan's words caused her terrible anxiety, seeming like a curse. They parted earlier than planned and promised to talk over the phone that night.

At 9 o'clock Xiaohui dialled several times before she heard Zhijun's voice. She hung up the phone immediately and went to Zhijun's home by taxi. The minute the door was closed, she and Zhijun embraced each other tightly.

His kisses and hugs excited her like an electric current. Her passion was aroused—a passion heightened by her suffering, a passion she had been longing for over the empty years. He was no longer the boy she had known. Their love-making was to be an entirely new experience. She lay nude and passive in front of him, her body perfectly toned from hours spent at the gym, a desperate, solitary body. He threw away his last piece of clothing and covered her tenderly like a warm quilt. All of a sudden, the phone rang. It continued ringing as they hungrily clung to each other. Their bodies became stiff and awkward just like frightened animals. The loud rings caused her passion to cool off. She said softly, "Go and answer the phone."

It was a long-winded call. She began to feel a chill through her whole body, and she had to cover herself with a blanket. Finally Zhijun sneaked under the blanket, too. His cold flesh made Xiaohui tremble. Silently he took up the cigarette and lighter on the nightstand.

"Was Yanyan calling?" she asked, looking at the ceiling.

"She said she was not feeling well and asked me to keep her company ..."

"Are you going? It's so late." She

turned over and glanced at him.

He puffed the cigarette gradually, and his face disappeared in the smoke, saying, "If I don't go, she will call me again and again. She has a mobile phone with her. And tonight she won't get to sleep."

She got up and put on her clothes. He took hold of her hand tightly.

"Xiaohui, I can ignore her. I'm well aware of her condition, and I'm sure nothing disastrous will happen to her tonight."

Xiaohui shook her head while putting on her socks, "But I'll be on edge the whole night ..." Before she finished her sentence, he sat up and held her in his arms from behind. He put his cheek against hers. His sudden tender affection made her shed tears freely.

She cried silently, and her tears

dropped on his arm. "Tell me, Xiaohui, do you have children?" he said, asking about her family for the first time.

She shook her head. Holding her more tightly, he said, "We'll both get a divorce and then get married." He said it hastily for fear of being cut short, "I have money. I've invested the money I earned in Japan in stocks, and I'm quite successful. I have enough money to buy a house. Xiaohui, we can live independently. We don't need to rely on anybody else. We'll have our child. Really, I often think you'll give birth to our child ..."

She smiled with tearful eyes, "Our child will be very pretty." She abruptly suppressed her smile and tears. She struggled out of his embrace and said facing him, "Why should we get a divorce? We can live together without getting a divorce. I can come back more often. I can buy a house in Shanghai. We'll live together for at least a couple of months every year, if you can come to Shanghai."

He didn't answer, but his expression became gloomy. She continued without evading his look, "I won't get a divorce. I belong to his family. My future and the prospects of my company depend on his family. It's not all about me either. In the past few years I've lived and breathed with them. We approach problems in the same way. We share the same hopes and worries. I'm a member of his family. How can I leave them just like that?"

He nodded his head and got up to dress himself, saying, "I was unable to persuade you to stay in Shanghai, and I'm unable to persuade you to come back to Shanghai. Xiaohui, I know I play a minor role in your life ..."

Xiaohui covered his mouth with her hand, saying, "You know that's not true. I've come to see you with the hope of spending more time with you in future. Maybe we will have a child of our own. If I start a company in Shanghai, I'll have enough time for a baby. I'm dying to have a child, but I'll only do it with the man I love."

"Xiaohui," he shouted in a serious mood, "your husband ... he ... is not capable ..."

"He is unable to help me produce a child. Actually, we sleep separately, in secret of course. He has a disease, but he's too busy with business to see a doctor." As soon as she had told him, she felt relieved. "I've got used to this kind of relationship—it's based on purely financial reasons. I couldn't even think about touching him ..." She smiled at herself, "This is the price I've paid. I bartered the life I dreamed of for my marriage."

"That's why you came to see me. Who do you take me for?" Zhijun said with a sneer.

"My lover, of course. What other role can you play?" Xiaohui stretched out her hand gloomily and put it in his. "Zhijun, since I often take business trips, I have my opportunities to find men." Drops of tears coursed down her face. "But I only want a lover. Zhijun, can't we be ... a holiday couple in Shanghai?"

Zhijun held his head in his hands and cried, saying, "How can we part again after we live together? I will treat you as my wife. How can I let you go back to Kuala Lumpur? Xiaohui, don't come back to me, if you don't intend to get a divorce ..."

At that moment, the dreadful ringing of the phone started again.

Two days later Xiaohui went to Hongqiao Airport by taxi. Just as she had come back to Shanghai on her own, she set off on the return journey alone with her luggage.

Her mother would be discharged from hospital the next day. She couldn't wait any longer because she didn't want to disappoint her husband any more than she had.

She didn't say good-bye to Zhang Lin, Qinghua or Zhen Zhen. She had left Zhijun's home and gone directly to Beijing Airport. She took a flight back to Shanghai. She went back to the hotel at midnight and slept for twelve hours straight. She woke up in the afternoon as if struggling her way out of a long dream. She spent the remaining hours with her mother.

While the taxi waited at a traffic light, she took out her cosmetic case. She looked at herself in the small mirror and found that her face was haggard with vivid rings around her eyes. During the seven days she had stayed in Shanghai, she seemed to be worn down by a terrible disease. It was quite gloomy outside as the rain was falling.

She put back her cosmetic case and looked through the gap in the protective glass. When she caught the driver's eye in the mirror—young black eyes—she flashed him a charming smile. He turned round and looked at her. He said with a smile, "I've taken a shortcut for you. Didn't you notice?" His teeth were solid and white.

"Oh, thank you. I don't know the way." She looked at her watch, "It's three hours before the departure time. You can make a detour. I'm not in a hurry ..."

The car started to move, but he fixed his eyes on her in the mirror.

"Aren't your family in Shanghai? How come nobody is seeing you off? And such a beautiful lady?" he asked.

She gazed out of the window intently. Quite a while later she answered, "Why don't you see me off? I've got three hours, and they're all yours." Her face was beaming.

"Do you want me to drive all the time?"

"It's too tiresome. We can sit in the café at the airport. Or, I have a good idea. We can go to a hotel near the airport. Usually they have some rooms free." She continued gazing out of the window.

The driver suddenly hit the brakes and said in a confused way, "I ... I have no time to spare ... I have to work my shift ... We're given a quota every day ..."

"How much?"

"About six hundred."

She counted out six one-hundred-yuan notes and gave them to him.

"You've fulfilled your quota for today."

"I ... have a wife. We're ... married ... for a year only ..." he said haltingly, without taking the money.

"It has nothing to do with marriage. I only want you to keep me company for three hours." She threw him a seductive smile as if she were a slut.

The car pulled out of Xinhua Road and drove onto Hongqiao Road, leading to the hotel.

Outside the international terminal building Xiaohui hurried out of the taxi. She went toward the green channel without looking back or halting her steps. Her newly made-up face looked fresh and brilliant, beaming with a faint smile.

Stories by Contemporary Writers from Shanghai

The Little Restaurant
Wang Anyi

A Pair of Jade Frogs
Ye Xin

Forty Roses
Sun Yong

Goodbye, Xu Hu!
Zhao Changtian

Vicissitudes of Life
Wang Xiaoying

The Elephant
Chen Cun

Folk Song
Li Xiao

The Messenger's Letter
Sun Ganlu

Ah, Blue Bird
Lu Xing'er

His One and Only
Wang Xiaoyu

When a Baby Is Born
Cheng Naishan

Dissipation
Tang Ying